# INVITATION

## DARCY BURKE

ZEALOUS QUILL PRESS

**Invitation**
Copyright © 2021 Darcy Burke
All rights reserved.
ISBN: 9781637260166

Book design: © Darcy Burke.
Book Cover Design: © Erin Dameron Hill.
Cover image: © Period Images.
Editing: Lindsey Faber.

❀ Created with Vellum

*For everyone who never got an invitation and wanted one.*

INVITATION

A PHOENIX CLUB SHORT STORY

**Society's most exclusive invitation...**

**Welcome to the Phoenix Club, where London's most audacious, disreputable, and intriguing ladies and gentlemen find scandal, redemption, and second chances.**

When Tobias Powell, the Viscount Deane, loses the young lady who's stolen his heart to a pompous heir to a dukedom, all of Society is abuzz with his failure. When a scandal further blackens his reputation, he decides to become the rogue everyone believes him to be.

When courtesan Mirabelle Renault's older sister marries her protector and is given the cut direct by the very Society who demands respectability, Mirabelle loses hope for her own future. Knowing she can no longer serve as a man's paramour, she is determined to forge a new path—until she realizes that most doors are closed to her.

Carefree bachelor Lord Lucien Westbrook has lost his mistress and gained his autocratic father's scrutiny now that his older brother is about to wed. Challenged to do something worthwhile, he launches an exclusive club, where Lucien helps those in need, no matter who they are or where they come from. One never knows who they will meet at the Phoenix Club…

Don't miss your next Regency obsession, *THE PHOENIX CLUB*!

Love romance? Have a free book (or two or three) on me!

Sign up at https://www.darcyburke.com/join for members-only exclusives, including advance notice of pre-orders and insider scoop, as well as contests, giveaways, freebies, and 99 cent deals!

Want to share your love of my books with like-minded readers? Want to hang with me and get inside scoop? Then don't miss my exclusive Facebook groups!

Darcy's Duchesses for historical readers
Burke's Book Lovers for contemporary readers

# CHAPTER 1

*April 1813, London*

*A*t the height of the London Season, nowhere was more rife with opportunity, scandal, and machination than Hyde Park. From the highest members of the ton to the lowliest footpad, there was something for everyone in this gathering place. Today, on this most glorious of afternoons, the colors of spring seemed more vibrant, the birdsong more melodious, and the smells of flowers, grass, and sunshine filled the air.

Tobias Powell, the Viscount Deane, grinned broadly at everyone he saw as he made his way into the park through the Grosvenor Gate. He didn't stop to speak with anyone as he was singularly focused on finding one particular person: his wife.

Rather, his soon-to-be wife.

People inclined their heads as Tobias walked past. Finding the dainty form of his beloved often proved difficult given her diminutive stature, but her face and figure were stamped indelibly in Tobias's mind. As were her sparkling laugh and keen interest in subjects ranging from art to birds to horses. She was the first and only young woman he'd met in Society who enjoyed discussing things beyond fashion, flowers, or food. She'd also demonstrated a fervent interest in something else—him. He had to admit that being with her was a heady drug, for she made him feel like the most important person in the world.

In front of him, people moved off the path and turned their backs. Tobias stopped short, frowning, wondering what the devil was going on. A couple walked toward him, the man's face tight and the woman… Well, the woman looked as if she were a breath away from bursting into tears. Her face was pale and her lower lip was drawn inward, as if she were biting the interior to keep her emotions in check.

Tobias suddenly realized what was happening. Everyone on the path was giving them the cut direct. Why? He had no idea who they were. No, wait, the gentleman looked vaguely familiar. In his early thirties, with thinning brown hair and sharp, sherry-colored eyes, he was a member at Brooks's. Despite that, he currently found himself on the nastier side of Society's capriciousness.

"Good afternoon," Tobias said warmly. He was in far too pleasant a mood to engage in such rude behavior, not that he would in any case.

"Afternoon, my lord," the gentleman said as a flicker of relief passed over his features. He patted the woman's hand where it rested on his sleeve, and they went along their way.

As Tobias continued along the path, two ladies who'd stepped to the side stared at him, their gazes holding a shadow of condescension. Oh, now they would disdain him—the heir to an earldom—for not being as judgmental as they were? He supposed that just went to show that no one was immune to the ton's whims.

He flashed them a wide grin. "Good afternoon, ladies. It's a rather lovely day, isn't it?"

One of them had the grace to look surprised before dipping her gaze to the ground. "Good afternoon, my lord."

Satisfied that he'd hopefully made at least one person rethink her behavior, he turned left onto another path toward the Serpentine. Lady Priscilla loved the water. She particularly enjoyed watching the waterfowl, for she enjoyed drawing them. He'd likely find her there.

Tobias quickened his pace, rehearsing what he planned to say in his head. He would declare his intent to call tomorrow morning in order to speak with her father. But first, he would obtain her answer—that was the most important thing. She would, of course, say yes. It was the clear culmination to their weeks-long courtship.

His father was going to be so pleased that Tobias would marry the daughter of a duke. He, of course, knew of Tobias's intent and wholeheartedly endorsed his choice.

"Deane!" a young buck called from just off the path where he stood with three other gentlemen.

Lifting his hand, Tobias waved. "Afternoon!"

Another of the gentlemen stepped to the edge of the path. "Too slow, then, or did she refuse you?"

A terrible chill raced through Tobias. He veered toward them, his pace slowing as his legs suddenly felt as though they were made of wood. "I beg your pardon?"

The last man who'd spoken, an old friend from school named Edwin Cleveland, moved away from the path, and the group widened to include Tobias.

"Lady Priscilla," Cleveland said. "Thought for sure you were going to bag her, but Bentley is the winner, it seems."

Bentley? Tobias felt as if he couldn't move or think. He knew Bentley was one of many who'd courted Lady Priscilla, but she'd been clear that her preference was for Tobias. Hadn't she? Doubt stole over him, and he didn't like the sensation one bit.

"You make it sound like a contest," Tobias said through an ever-deepening disappointment. Except that word didn't begin to describe what he felt. He'd *loved* her. He'd expected to marry her in a month's time. A year from now, they likely would have been parents. He couldn't breathe.

Another of the gentleman snorted. "It *is* a contest. One winner, many losers. You're a loser this time, Deane."

Cleveland sniffed. "At least he outranks you. Would have been deuced awful to lose to someone lesser."

In Tobias's mind, Bentley *was* someone lesser. The man was a cheat at cards and took every opportunity to inflate his own importance. That Lady Priscilla would choose him over Tobias... It was unconscionable.

He wanted to know why. Was it really because of rank? Bentley barely outranked him. Furthermore, Tobias's father's earldom was older, and, as far as Tobias knew, their estate was larger.

Hell, none of that should matter. It was only important that they suit, and Tobias believed that he and Lady Priscilla were perfectly suited.

"You didn't know," the first gentleman who'd called out to Tobias said in wonder, his dark gaze fixed on Tobias. "You didn't know she'd chosen Bentley."

Tobias clenched his jaw and said nothing.

Cleveland winced, then laughed. "Oh, bad luck that."

"At least you heard it from us," the fourth man said with a chuckle. "Imagine if you'd proposed and she had to refuse you."

"Yes, imagine," another of them said—Tobias stopped

paying attention to who. He could only see red. He was angry, humiliated, hurt...

"Excuse me," he murmured before taking himself off, turning back the way he'd come.

He walked twice as fast as when he'd been eager to find the woman he'd expected would be his wife. When he turned toward the Grosvenor Gate, he was painfully aware of the sudden attention directed at him, and the talk that was just loud enough so that he could hear his name and that of Lady Priscilla. News of her engagement was spreading like a plague.

No one turned their back on him, for this wasn't the cut direct such as he'd witnessed earlier. It was, however, another cruelty Society inflicted as it took one person's heartache or scandal and devoured it like a cheesecake.

He left the park as quickly as possible and immediately caught a hack to St. James Street, specifically Brooks's Club, where he could drown himself in a large glass of brandy. As he entered the subscription room, he wondered if any of the gentlemen there had already heard the news. Not that it mattered. In this gentlemen's haven, no one would trouble him about losing out to Bentley.

Oh hell, now *he* was thinking of it like a contest.

Wasn't it, though? Bentley had won, and Tobias had definitely lost. Lady Priscilla would not be his wife. He couldn't even fight for her, not without causing a scandal.

But what if Lady Priscilla really did prefer him? What if she wanted him to rescue her from a marriage she didn't desire? He could whisk her away to Gretna Green...

He walked past the tables where men were playing cards and went into a smaller antechamber where his favorite table was located. He nearly choked when he saw his father seated there.

The earl met Tobias's gaze. His expression reflected nothing but the placid indifference he typically wore.

Tobias wasn't sure what to expect. On one hand, he hoped his father already knew about Lady Priscilla, for then Tobias wouldn't have to tell him. On the other, he didn't want his father to know he'd lost. He would know, however. There would be no hiding it from him.

"Sit," the earl said.

Taking the chair to his father's left, Tobias lowered himself between the dark wood arms. He did not relax. "I'm surprised to see you here at this time of day."

"As you should be. I don't dawdle about when there is important work to be done." The earl referred to his position in the House of Lords where he chaired a few important committees. "Hadleigh informed me his daughter is to marry Bentley. Imagine *my* surprise at hearing that news."

Tobias gritted his teeth and clutched the arms of the chair. "I only just heard it myself. At the park."

The earl's smoke-colored eyes, nearly the same hue as his mostly gray hair, narrowed. "I suppose you must move on to the next chit on your list."

Forcing his hands to relax, Tobias flexed his fingers. "I don't have a list."

"How disappointing. Fortunately, I do." He withdrew a small piece of paper from his coat and slid it along the tablecloth toward Tobias. "They are in order of my preference. I have already spoken to Lord Billingsworth, and he is amenable to your suit. Lady Agnes is not the daughter of a duke, but she is at least the daughter of an earl."

She was also simpering and couldn't be bothered to speak of anything beyond the three Fs: fashion, flowers, and food. Actually, that wasn't true. She was also eager to discuss the latest on-dit. Tobias couldn't think of a worse match.

He looked at the paper as if it might burn him if he touched it. "No."

"No?" The earl exhaled. "There are other names on the list if you can't muster the appropriate enthusiasm for Lady Agnes. Though you must admit, she fills out a gown quite nicely."

Tobias cringed. "Father, please refrain from making such comments about anyone you'd like me to take to wife."

Not a moment too soon, the footman delivered a glass of Tobias's preferred brandy. Tobias took a long sip and briefly closed his eyes as the delectable heat soothed his irritation.

"I'm sure you'll find someone who will suit. I expect a proposal within the week." The earl leaned toward him, the gray of his eyes crystallizing to ice. "Do *not* disappoint me again."

As the earl started to rise, Tobias whispered, "I loved her."

"What's that?" his father asked a bit crossly.

"I said I loved her. I don't think I can summon the interest—or emotion—to propose to anyone else within the next week, let alone this Season."

As he dropped back into his chair, the earl's mouth tightened. "You listen to me, now. Interest and emotion aren't required. Duty is all you must consider and the only thing that matters. Take the list."

Reluctantly, his anger rising to the surface once more, Tobias picked the paper up and tucked it into his coat. "Satisfied?"

"Not until I hear the bells of St. Paul's chiming on your wedding day." The earl gave Tobias a sharp stare before standing and leaving the room.

"Brilliant," Tobias muttered. He noted a pair of gentlemen at the next table staring at him.

One of the men raised his glass. "Condolences, Deane. Better luck next time!" He laughed, and his tablemate joined in the chorus.

Biting back a curse, Tobias swept up his glass and abruptly stood. He'd find a private alcove where no one would bother him.

Except as soon as he went back into the subscription room, he nearly ran into two of his closest friends.

"Drinking already?" Lord Lucien Westbrook asked. "Good."

"Come." Ruark Hannigan, Lord Wexford, clapped his hand on Tobias's shoulder.

They led him upstairs to Lucien's father's private chamber. The Duke of Evesham had one of the finest private rooms in the club, not that he ever used it. He preferred the more conservative air of White's.

"Why does your father still keep this room?" Ruark asked in his lilting Irish accent, closing the door behind him. The dark wood and deep blue hues of the chamber's décor declared this to be a masculine space, while the paintings by Hogarth and Reynolds and the thick Aubusson carpet demonstrated opulence.

Lucien shrugged as he crossed the chamber. "Because he can. Aldington uses it occasionally."

The earl was Lucien's staid older brother.

Ruark flashed a brilliant smile that never failed to make young ladies swoon. He would be the most sought after bachelor in town if not for his Irishness. "He should be more comfortable at White's too."

Lucien arrived at the sideboard, where he poured two glasses of brandy. "I don't think he's comfortable anywhere. Awfully hard when you've a stick up your arse."

Ruark laughed, and Tobias found himself smiling despite the afternoon's revelations.

"Thank you," Tobias said before taking another sip of brandy and throwing himself in a sturdy, high-backed chair adjacent to the fireplace.

"Don't mope," Lucien said as he took another chair—there were several scattered about the room, with four relatively near the hearth, including the one he now inhabited. "Act as if you never cared a whit for her."

Tobias appreciated his friend's support and his advice. "You know I did."

"What is real and what you present to the world do not have to be the same thing."

Ruark lifted his glass to his lips and murmured, "Said the former spy," before taking a drink.

Lucien rolled his eyes. He'd returned from Spain just a few months prior after serving under Wellington. "I was not a spy. If I was, don't you think I'd still be there?"

"Just jesting with you." Ruark was ever the wit.

"Everyone is talking about my rejection," Tobias said evenly, despite the anger and disappointment welling inside him once more. "I made no secret of the seriousness of my courtship."

"This will pass," Ruark said encouragingly. "Soon, you won't even remember her name, nor what she looks like."

"That's what my father would prefer. He's instructed me to propose to someone else with due haste. Even gave me a list."

"What a bloody nuisance," Ruark muttered. "You poor blokes with your meddling, dictatorial fathers. I'll count myself lucky I don't have one anymore." He gave them a smug smile.

Tobias grunted into his glass before tossing the rest down his gullet. "I need more brandy."

Lucien obliged, fetching the bottle and refilling Tobias's glass. "When you finish that, I've just the gaming hell to distract you."

Yes, distraction was good. Tobias lifted his brandy. "I'll drink to that."

# CHAPTER 2

*M*irabelle Renault watched in agitation as her older sister trailed back and forth across the small parlor of Mirabelle's lodgings. What should have been a happy, triumphant day, Heloise's first outing in Society since becoming Mrs. Alfred Creighton a fortnight ago, had instead been a disaster.

"I don't understand. I did precisely what Society demands. I married well!" Heloise paused, wringing her hands as her gaze darted to her husband, who looked on from his chair with love and support.

"That is not enough for some," Alfred said softly. "I don't care, my love. Let them think what they must. They are the ones trapped by their own stupid rules."

Heloise's light brown curls swung against her neck as she resumed pacing. "Stupid indeed. What are we to do now?" She stopped again and fixed her anguished gaze on her husband.

A strident fury rose in Mirabelle. She and Heloise had done what they must to survive, and that Heloise had risen from their awful circumstances and found not just love, but respectability and security was a testament to her determination—and her warm heart.

Alfred shifted in his chair, the light from the sconce on the wall glinting off the thinning patch of hair atop his head. Six years older than Heloise's twenty-five, he'd never been married and had fallen deeply in love with his mistress. So in love that he'd married her. "We'll remove to the country," he said.

Heloise sank onto the settee beside Mirabelle, her shoulders drooping in defeat. "But we just returned from Nottinghamshire yesterday."

"I thought you liked it there," Alfred noted, his brows shooting up.

"I loved it," Heloise said softly. She turned her head toward Mirabelle. "Truly, I've never felt more at home. It reminds me of how Mama used to describe our house in France."

They'd been born in the countryside, not that either of them remembered it. Heloise had been three and Mirabelle just a babe when they'd emigrated to England with their mother and her maid. Their father, a chevalier, had been killed in the revolution.

"I look forward to visiting it someday," Mirabelle said, despite never feeling a pull toward France or the country-side or anything else their mother had talked about. Prob-ably because Mirabelle didn't remember her. She'd died when Mirabelle was three, and they'd been raised by Nadine, their mother's maid, who'd cared for them in their cramped but cozy lodgings near Compton Street in Soho.

"You are welcome to come with us now," Alfred said. He'd generously offered to bring Mirabelle into their household so that she would no longer have to be a para-mour. Mirabelle had followed her sister into the same profession after Nadine's death. The choice between seamstress and courtesan was easy when one considered the opportunities available to the latter. A seamstress's life might be more reliable, but it was long, hard work for little pay.

Furthermore, Mirabelle wasn't particularly skilled with a needle. Not like Nadine had been.

Mirabelle gave her brother-in-law an appreciative smile. "Thank you, but I can't see myself living anywhere but London." It was the only home she'd ever known. Indeed, she'd never even lived outside Soho.

"I do hope you'll come visit," Heloise said. "Particularly since it looks as though we'll be living there permanently."

Mirabelle took her sister's hand in a fierce grip. "I'm so sorry. But listen to your husband. In the end, it doesn't matter what these people think of you. Go to Nottinghamshire where you will be happy. Promise me you'll be happy." She needed Heloise to do that. One of them had to be.

"I promise." Heloise leaned her head toward Mirabelle and whispered, "And you will be too."

Heloise's disappointment and ire stayed with Mirabelle long after she and Alfred left. Anger still simmered when her lover strode into the parlor. Mirabelle stood at the window and spared him only a brief glance.

"You're upset." Lucien moved to the cabinet where she kept her wine and spirits. He brought her a glass of sherry. "What's the trouble?"

Mirabelle turned from the window and snatched the glass from him, nearly sloshing sherry over the side. "Your bloody Society. Nasty vipers, the lot of them."

"Agreed." He slipped his arm around her waist. His familiar touch, warm and steady, did nothing to soothe her.

She sipped her sherry and walked away from his

embrace. His silence prompted her to turn. He stood in the same place, his brow furrowed beneath the wave of dark hair crowning his forehead. With his exceptional height, broad shoulders, and nearly black, piercing gaze, he presented an intimidating figure and a commanding presence. He was also sin incarnate.

Lucien wasn't her first protector, but he was by far the best, and not just because of his skills in the bedchamber. He was considerate, caring, and, most importantly, he treated her like an equal person whose thoughts and opinions mattered to him.

Pushing out a breath, Mirabelle strolled to her favorite chair near the hearth. Orange coals burned, radiating a warmth that didn't permeate her exterior. "My sister and her husband visited earlier. They were given the cut direct at Hyde Park today."

A colorful epithet darted from Lucien's mouth. Mirabelle stared at his lips a moment—they were far more beautiful than a man deserved, lush and soft, almost feminine, except the sharp edge of his jaw and angular lines of his cheekbones kept them from being so. She was going to miss feeling them on her body.

She lifted her chin and looked him in the eye. "I want you to go."

He strode toward her, stopping a foot or so away. "Let me stay. I'll help you forget about Society's nonsense."

Gripping her sherry glass, Mirabelle hardened her gaze. "Is it nonsense when it's my sister's very life? She did precisely as she should—she married one of *you*. She elevated herself to a position of respectability."

His jaw clenched. "Not all of Society are like the harridans in the park."

"Far more of the ton are like them than like you." She

sipped her sherry, but it did nothing to alleviate her irritation.

"Which is why you choose to spend your time with me." His tempting lips curled into a satisfied smile. He moved forward, lessening the space between them.

Mirabelle skirted him and walked back to the window. "I spend my time with you because that's what you pay me for." She heard his intake of breath but didn't turn. Instead, she stared out the window and fixed on the lamp across the street.

"That's all I am to you?"

She knew he cared for her, as much as a protector could care for the woman who warmed his bed but with whom he would never share a lasting relationship. Perhaps not *never*. Heloise had found that one-in-a-million gentleman who'd truly fallen in love with her. He'd seen the woman beneath the courtesan, the vulnerable girl who'd been forced from her home and scraped to survive in a foreign land.

While Lucien saw those things too, it was different. He didn't love her. Nor did Mirabelle love him. She did like him, though.

Pivoting halfway from the window, she glanced in his direction. "You are more than that. A friend, I hope. But that is all. I don't want this life anymore."

She'd been considering it for a while now, but hadn't realized she'd made the decision until the words tumbled forth. Heloise's experience today had starkly illustrated what would happen in the very best of circumstances.

"You want to break things off with me?"

"Yes, and I don't wish to engage in an arrangement with another gentleman again. Ever. I am tired of living on the fringe, of wondering if I should have stayed a poor seamstress and tried to work my way into a finer shop in Mayfair."

"I've seen your attempts at embroidery, Belle. I can't see you as a modiste." The humor in Lucien's tone should have made her smile, but she was just...cold.

"Just because I can't sew doesn't mean I can't manage others who do."

He laughed, and the sound was the first thing that had given her a modicum of comfort besides the sherry. "*That* I can imagine. You are a managing sort. Indeed, I could see you in charge of a grand house with an army of servants and a half dozen children."

She pursed her lips at him. "Please tell me that isn't a proposal. It was extremely unromantic."

He came toward her, but stopped after a few steps. "May I approach?" He eyed her with hesitation and perhaps a ray of hope.

"You may."

When he was close, but not too close, he took her free hand, clasping it gently between his thumb and fingers. "I would never deign to offer for your hand. I am not worthy."

She let out a most unladylike snort. "Your father would say *I* am not worthy."

"True, but he has exceptionally poor taste." Lucien flashed a smile, then pressed a kiss to her hand before letting her go. "If you aren't to continue in this life, as you put it, what do you plan to do?"

"I'm considering my options." She had absolutely no idea. It was both terrifying and exhilarating. She had a bit of money saved, but not enough to open her own modiste shop.

He arched a dark brow, the glow of hope in his gaze brightening. "Would you consider a separation gift from me that would see you settled wherever and however you'd like?"

"Absolutely not. You should know me better than that. I don't take charity."

"I'd say you earned it."

"That isn't much better. You've already compensated me more extravagantly than most women in my trade can expect."

He lifted a shoulder. "I can afford it."

Mirabelle let out a low grunt and stalked away from him again. "Oh, just go. You're no better than them, tossing around your importance and your wealth. I don't need either of those things. I'll provide for myself, thank you, just as I have always done."

"Your pride is a marvelous thing. Please don't let it get the better of you."

She swung around to face him, and this time, sherry did crest over the side of the glass and splash her fingers. "Spoken like a man who doesn't understand the meaning of privilege or what it means not to have any. Please go. I'll be gone from here within the week."

He frowned, the muscles in his jaw working. "Belle."

"Please go." She turned her back on him, her body thrumming with an inner turmoil that she now realized had been building for some time.

She knew Lucien had left—the air in a room always changed with his presence, or lack thereof. Closing her eyes briefly, she exhaled.

Then she wondered just what in the hell she was going to do.

# CHAPTER 3

"Good afternoon, brother." Lady Cassandra Westbrook swanned into the entrance hall just after Lucien stepped inside. Her dark hair was swept into the latest style, and her warm brown eyes assessed him with a precision that never failed to unnerve him. She was too smart—smarter than all of them by far.

He glanced up toward the first floor. "What, were you watching for my arrival from your sitting room?"

"I was looking out the window, yes. And of course I would come down to see you. I know you won't linger after your meeting with Father."

No, he would not. He hated these summonses with a fiery passion. "You'll see me Friday morning for our usual ride."

"True." She frowned in the direction of their father's study. "How I wish I could be invited to one of your interviews."

Lucien chuckled. "No, you don't, trust me."

"It will never happen anyway. I am not a *son*." She said the last word with a deep, pretentious tone that was clearly to mimic their father. As Lucien started to turn, she added, "Pale yellow isn't much of a statement. I rather prefer the chartreuse."

Long ago, Lucien had discovered how much their father despised any deviation from conservative attire. Wearing a non-white cravat in the duke's presence was a small act of rebellion, but one Lucien would cling to as long as he drew breath. He smiled at his sister. "Then I shall be certain to wear it next time."

A few moments later, he walked into his father's large study with its dark, towering bookcases and heavy, midnight-blue draperies cloaking the bank of windows that looked out to Grosvenor Square.

"Yellow, really?" Lucien's older brother, Constantine, stood near the hearth, over which hung an awful portrait of their father with a half dozen hunting dogs. The duke gripped his gun and held a dead fox by the scruff.

Lucien gaped at the painting, ignoring Con's jibe. "Is *this* what he had commissioned?"

"Apparently." The single word curled with disgust.

"At least we share an opinion on the repulsiveness of that...piece." They typically didn't agree on much of anything. Lucien moved to stand near the windows, his gaze drifting to his coach waiting for him to escape at the earliest possible opportunity.

"Good, you're both here." The duke strode into the study and went straight to his massive desk, which sat opposite the windows. He paused before taking his chair and frowned at Lucien's cravat.

Lucien quashed a satisfied smirk.

The duke sat, his almost entirely gray head tipping toward the hunting portrait. "I see you're observing the new painting. Magnificent, isn't it?"

Exchanging a dubious look with his brother, Lucien didn't respond, while Con said, "Quite."

While Lucien and his father were dark-eyed and dark-haired—the duke's hair had once been sable—Con was a lighter version of them. With tawny brown hair and green-brown eyes, he'd inherited their mother's classic bone structure. He was also quieter, as she had been, leaving Lucien and the duke to butt heads.

"Is that why you invited us today?" Lucien walked to a chair and sat down, extending his legs out in front of him. "To fawn over your portrait?" He kept his gaze fixed on the duke.

"No. Aldington didn't tell you the purpose?" The duke used Con's courtesy title. As a young boy, Lucien had found it too long and cumbersome to say, so he'd called his brother Con. Their sister Cass had done the same thing.

Con, dressed impeccably in somber colors and a pristinely white cravat, briefly massaged the bridge of his nose. "I didn't. Lucien only just arrived, Father." Exhaling, Con pivoted to face his brother. "I'm to be wed." His gaze flicked to their father, ever seeking his approval. That right there told Lucien everything, that Con was doing his duty and nothing more.

Lucien wished that surprised him. Instead, it just made him sad. "Your joy is wonderfully evident," he cracked. "Who is the lucky lady?"

"Lady Sabrina Kidd." Con didn't even *sound* enthused.

"Bloody hell, man, can't you muster a modicum of emotion?" Lucien asked.

Con scowled at him. "I'm very much looking forward to marrying her. She'll make an excellent duchess. At some point in the future."

Yes, that was all that mattered, that Con choose

someone worthy of being a duchess. Emotion—love, passion, even like—had nothing to do with it. "Do you even realize you're frowning?" Lucien asked.

Con repositioned his body toward their father once more so that Lucien could only see him in profile. It was still evident, however, that Con was making an effort to at least look...not pained.

Poor Lady Sabrina.

Lucien had met her. Hell, he may have even danced with her at one point. He tried to summon Lady Sabrina in her mind. She was blonde, perhaps? A bit taller than average? Honestly, he couldn't recall her. He fixed Con with a probing stare. "What is it about her that provoked you to marriage?"

Again, Con darted a look toward their father, and it was all Lucien could do not to grab his brother by the shoulders and shake him until something inside him gave way. "She's demure and kind, excellent at the pianoforte." He paused, and Lucien folded his arms expectantly. "She, ah, likes dogs," Con added. "And she's the daughter of the Viscount Tarleton."

"Oh, well, that seals it, then." Lucien uncrossed his arms and resisted the urge to roll his eyes. If his brother were to wed, Lucien wanted him to do it because *he* wanted to, not because their father had demanded it. But Con had always bowed to their father's wishes. As the duke said—and Con parroted—it was the duty of the heir to do as he must, not as he chose. Lucien should have done more to push his brother into some semblance of freedom. The man should have at least chosen his own bloody wife. Alas, here they were. "My deepest congratulations for your wedded bliss." Lucien stood, grateful for the short interview.

"Sit." The duke leveled his signature commanding stare

at Lucien. Though he was no longer intimidated by his father, Lucien always chose the path of least resistance with him. So he sat back down.

Father clasped his hands atop his desk. "Now that Aldington is to wed, you will need to do the same."

"Someday, I shall." It was nowhere in any of Lucien's current plans nor would it be.

"Not someday. *Soon.* I won't force you." As if he could. "My hope is that you will do so by the end of next Season. If you'd like a list of acceptable young ladies, including those who are not yet out but will be next year, I'll provide one." What was it with fathers and bride lists?

Lucien summoned a placid expression. "Is that what you did for Con?" He sent a pitying look toward his brother. "I'm sure I can manage."

"I'll be the judge of that. I would prefer to have input into your choice, but I daresay you won't allow me that fatherly duty." He sniffed in a weak attempt at appearing offended.

It wasn't a bloody *duty* to meddle in your son's, especially your second son's, marital affairs.

"No, I will not. It isn't your duty to choose my wife, *or* Con's." Lucien glared toward his brother. "Dammit, Con, why do you let him control everything?"

Con's answering stare was frigid. "I don't. You seem to think I don't make decisions for myself, but I do. Just because you don't agree with them doesn't mean they're wrong. For a younger brother, you are annoyingly meddlesome."

Stung, Lucien sat back in his chair and blew out a breath. Was he no better than their father, trying to manage Con? Was Lucien's irritation at Con's impending marriage to do with Con at all, or was it due to the fact that their father's focus would now shift completely to

Lucien? The pressure to wed would be applied most vocif-
erously.

"I shall do my best to select someone acceptable,"
Lucien responded, though he was thinking he'd do just the
opposite to spite him.

The duke's answering expression was one of heavy
skepticism. "What's important for now is that you mend
your libidinous ways. Your reputation requires rehabilita-
tion if you hope to make the best possible marriage."

Lucien wiped his hand over his face, thoroughly weary
of this interview. "I served under Wellington and received
a medal. What more could I do to improve my reputation?"

"Stop gallivanting about town with your unending
parade of mistresses. Stop spending so much time in
gaming hells. Attend more Society events. And most
importantly—do something with your life." He put his
elbows on the desk and steepled his hands. "You should
have stood for the Commons last autumn."

That had been a massive battle that had resulted in
Lucien not speaking to his father until well into the new
year. "It's not enough that Con is already a member?
Besides, I'd only been home from Spain a month."

"Closer to two, but let's not quibble. You would have
been elected easily." *Any* gentleman with money was
elected easily because he could afford the bribes necessary to win. For that reason alone, Lucien wasn't
interested.

He rose again, checking his watch fob. "I must be off."
He turned to Con and inclined his head. "Felicitations to
you and Lady Sabrina. When is the wedding?"

"Early June."

"I'll look forward to it." As he walked nearer to his
brother, Lucien added in a near whisper, "And I hope you
will too."

Lucien lifted his hand toward the duke. "Afternoon, Father. Thank you, as always, for your counsel."

"One more thing," the duke said sharply, halting Lucien's departure. "I've given up my private chamber at Brooks's. I see no need for it since I rarely ever visit."

Though Lucien couldn't see his father's face, the derision in his tone was blatantly evident. Barely pivoting, Lucien glanced back toward him. "I go there nearly every night. Surely you know that."

"Do you?" Though the duke sounded as though he had no idea, Lucien knew better.

There would be no point in trying to persuade him to keep it, nor would Lucien lower himself to ask. This was a minor punishment for not falling into line. No matter, Lucien would find a cozy alcove to meet with his friends. Or maybe he'd do something else entirely. Hell, his mistress was leaving him, and now his gathering place had been stripped away too.

Without another word, Lucien stalked from the study. Before he reached the entrance hall, Con caught up to him.

"Would it kill you to improve your behavior?"

Lucien reluctantly slowed as his brother came abreast of him. "Would it kill *you* to relax a bit and enjoy life?"

Con brushed at something on his sleeve. "Just because we do not share the same…passions doesn't mean I do not enjoy life."

Lucien stopped and turned to face his brother, folding his arms over his chest. "Passions?" He waggled his brows. "Dare I hope you've developed a tendre for your bride? Perhaps you haven't repressed *everything*."

"Must you debase every conversation?"

"Well, I don't, but I *could*." Lucien grinned, then uncrossed his arms, letting them drop to his sides. "My apologies, brother. I should not taunt you. You make it too easy. But that does not mean you're inviting me to torment you."

Con's eyes darkened. "You've skirted the issue, Luci." Only his siblings called him by the nickname. "Please, give a thought to your reputation—your standing, if not your family."

"Are you honestly concerned my behavior will cause you to suffer?"

"No, but think of our sister."

Lucien glanced toward the entrance hall, where he'd seen Cassandra earlier. "Is there a problem?"

"Well...no. But how would we know if there were?"

Rolling his eyes, Lucien turned toward the foyer. "She's not even out, for heaven's sake. Stop trying to stir trouble where there is none. You are becoming more like Father every day."

Con clenched his jaw. "If you kept your...activities more private and didn't flaunt your dissipation, it would be far more tolerable. Can't you find something worthwhile to do?"

"Worthwhile is subjective, Constantine," Lucien said softly but with a touch of heat.

He took his leave and drove back to his small bachelor house on King Street near St. James Square. Con's marriage would invite more meddling from their father, as evidenced today. The duke hadn't only *not* persuaded Lucien to remedy his behavior, he'd rather done the opposite. Lucien was more encouraged than ever to carouse and debauch, particularly since he was suddenly in the market for a new mistress.

Frowning as he turned toward Piccadilly, he thought of Mirabelle. He'd hoped she would change her mind or that she hadn't actually been serious. But of course she had been. Furthermore, she'd sent him a note that morning indicating she'd found lodgings and would be moving in a few days. Lucien wanted to ask where, to ensure she would be safe and comfortable, but it wasn't his place to ask. She'd been clear about leaving her profession and claiming her independence.

He also knew she didn't have another trade to fall back on.

Frustration drove him back to his conversation with his brother. *Intolerable?* Was that how Con saw him? Of all the judgmental, pompous...

But wasn't that also how Lucien saw his brother? The duke had done an excellent job of pitting them against each other. At least that was how it seemed to Lucien. Or perhaps it was just that they were that different, that being the heir and being the spare created a rift.

Lucien shook out his shoulders before he grew too tense. His father, and by extension his brother, didn't like the company he kept—either his friends or his women. Nor did they like that he preferred Brooks's to White's or supported *liberal* ideas such as election reform. It was apparently blasphemous to think all men, and even women, should be able to vote and that anyone should be able to run for office.

Worse than blasphemous, it was *intolerable*.

Lucien turned his thoughts to Tobias, who, like Mirabelle's sister, was also suffering from Society's nastiness. During his morning ride on Rotten Row, Lucien had overheard several gentlemen discussing Bentley's victory with the apparently popular Lady Priscilla. They didn't seem to realize, or care, that Tobias's heart had been broken.

Lucien cared. Just as he cared for Mirabelle and what she was going to do. His brother's words rose in his mind: *Can't you find something worthwhile to do?*

In fact, he rather thought he might be able to do just that.

# CHAPTER 4

$\mathcal{L}$ady Priscilla was the only reason Tobias had come to the Oxley ball. He clung to the shadows as much as possible, both to avoid running into his father and to keep from sparking interest in his presence. The ton was still abuzz with his loss and, perhaps more accurately, fixated on Bentley's victory.

Tobias had seen him shortly after he'd arrived, preening in the center of a group of ardent admirers, both male and female. The heir to a dukedom was always seen as a good ally, even when they were self-important dullards.

Not long after that, Tobias had finally caught sight of Lady Priscilla. Her light brown hair was piled atop her head in curls woven through with a silver ribbon and jewels. She wore a pale blue gown that elegantly draped her petite form. A pang of longing had shot through him, and he hoped his plan wouldn't be for naught.

He watched while she sipped ratafia with other ladies. After some time, she departed the ballroom in the company of her mother.

This was the moment he'd been planning for. Hopefully, they were on their way to the retiring room, because the scheme he'd engineered depended on it. Seeing that was, in fact, their destination, Tobias exhaled with relief. He lingered nearby, his body thrumming with nervous energy as he waited to see if his plan would work.

A few moments later, Lady Priscilla came back out just as he'd hoped she would. Tobias strode quickly to her and gently touched her back. "Lady Priscilla, might I have a word?"

"Lord Deane?" Her eyes lit with surprise and something else. Pleasure, perhaps. There was also a shadow of confusion. "The maid said Bentley needed to speak with me."

"That's what I paid her to say, yes." Tobias tried not to sound impatient, but if someone happened upon them, the entire scheme would be finished before it even began. "Will you come with me?"

She nodded. "I'm quite pleased to see you, actually. I was afraid you'd be angry." She looked up at him tentatively as he guided her to the sitting room several paces away. "Are you?"

"No, of course not. Well, not anymore." After ushering her into the sitting room, he closed the door firmly. It was too bad there wasn't a lock. Due to the threat of discovery, he took just two steps into the room so he would be able to hear if anyone approached. "I was shocked to learn you'd become betrothed to Bentley. I thought we suited quite well."

She turned to face him, her pale brows knitted. "I'm so sorry. You must understand that my parents preferred Bentley's suit."

Exactly as he'd suspected. "I did wonder what happened. I'd planned to propose to you yesterday afternoon, then to speak with your father this morning. I suppose it's my bad luck that Bentley got to you both first."

She stepped closer to him. "I'm not sure it would have mattered. My father was quite set on Bentley."

Tobias edged toward her so that they nearly touched. "And were you set on someone? In particular?"

Pink swathed her cheeks, and her lashes fluttered as she glanced away. "I tried not to be, but I admit I preferred you to Bentley." She returned her gaze to his, an expectant smile lifting her mouth.

Happiness swelled in Tobias's chest. "I'd thought so." He clasped her fingers and pressed his lips to her knuckles. Clutching her hand to his chest, he stared into her eyes. "It's not too late for us to be together. We can leave for Gretna Green right now."

Her jaw dropped, but she clutched his fingers. "That would be madness!" She sounded breathless, and her blue eyes sparkled with excitement.

He took her reaction to mean she wasn't opposed to the idea, but that it was risky. "It's the only solution left to us, unless you think your father can be persuaded to allow you to refuse Bentley."

Her forehead creased with concern. "My father did not ask whom I preferred to marry. I don't think he can be deterred from Bentley. In any case, that would be a scandal at this point. Our betrothal is public knowledge."

"Dashing off to Gretna Green will also be a scandal." Tobias stroked his thumb along the side of her hand. "I await your direction, my lady."

She turned her head, her brow puckering and her lips pursing. "I am so confused. I do like you more than Bentley. And this is such a grand, romantic gesture." Her expression brightened, and she brought her other hand up to clasp his between hers. "How can I refuse you?"

She *liked* him? A chill raced through Tobias. Like was not love.

The sound of voices outside the door jolted Tobias into action. He looked wildly about the room for a place to hide. Holding her hand tightly, he pulled her behind the heavy draperies at the window, grateful they were both voluminous and thick.

"What are you—"

Tobias clapped his hand over her mouth. "Shhh. Someone is coming," he whispered urgently.

The click of the door opening followed by the snick of it closing made Tobias hold his breath. The voices started again, and he strained to listen.

"This is cozy," said a woman, her voice low and provocative. Oh God, were he and Lady Priscilla about to overhear an assignation?

"Indeed," the man purred.

There was no mistaking the sounds of kissing, at least not for Tobias. And here he was, squeezed into a small, dark place with the woman he loved pressed against his chest. Her floral scent suddenly assaulted him, stirring a thoroughly inconvenient desire.

Lady Priscilla flattened her palms against his chest. "It sounds like they're kissing," she whispered.

He put his hands on her waist and tried to keep from pulling her hips to his. "Don't talk."

"All right." Then her lips were on his, and the longing inside him unfurled into a fiery lust. He splayed his palms over her lower back and brought her flush against his erection. They'd kissed before, but not with this sense of desperation, of utter need. Perhaps that was because he thought he'd lost her.

Her tongue licked along his lips before slipping into his mouth. Holy hell, where had she learned to do that?

Bentley, probably.

Lifting his head, Tobias clasped her waist and held her

apart from him. Then he listened intently, but the room was silent.

"Did they leave?" she murmured.

Tobias waited a few moments. Upon hearing nothing, save the rapid beat of his heart, he pivoted, careful not to move the drape, and peered around the edge. The room was empty.

He exhaled as he let her go and quickly left the shield of the draperies. "That was a near thing."

"*That* would have been a scandal for certain." She giggled. "Gretna Green would not have been necessary then, just a special license." She sucked in a breath, drawing Tobias to turn to her in fear. She did not look afraid. She appeared...titillated. "Perhaps Bentley would have called you out! Is there anything more romantic than having two men fight a duel over your hand?"

Only that wasn't what Tobias would be doing. He'd be defending his—and her—honor. That she was intensely thrilled by this prospect filled him with dread. "A duel is the furthest thing from romantic."

Her eyes widened. "Oh! Well, yes, I suppose so. I only meant that I would feel honored that you both care so much. It is rather wonderful to be so highly desired." She smiled prettily, her gaze raking over him with unabashed appreciation. "But surely *you* know that."

Tobias felt queasy. Society had been right to laugh at him. He'd been an utter fool. He'd fallen in love with this young woman who apparently *liked* him well enough, but who was perhaps in love with being wanted and not with any gentleman in particular. She'd made him feel special—the way she'd just looked at him and flattered him. Had she treated Bentley the same way? Tobias assumed she had.

The words contest, win, and lose came back to him.

Perhaps this was all just a game, even to the young woman before him.

"Lady Priscilla, I fear my scheme to spirit you away to Gretna Green is a foolhardy one. We would most certainly be caught, and it would cause a terrible scandal. Indeed, I never should have brought you in here. The risk to your reputation is too great. Please accept my deepest apologies."

Her mouth drooped as she took a step toward him. He quickly moved back.

"You've changed your mind?" she asked, sounding so disappointed that he nearly reversed his decision. Again.

"I've come to my senses," he said definitively. "You are already betrothed. The marriage contract has probably been signed." Hell, why hadn't he thought of that before? Because he'd been an utter dunderhead. "You should return to the retiring room. Your mother may have missed you by now."

As it was, they were already supposed to have been on their way. The arrival of the amorous couple had ruined the timing of his plan, even if Tobias hadn't suffered a change of heart.

Had he? Was his heart free of Lady Priscilla?

She stepped forward and hastily stood on her toes to press a kiss to his cheek. "I did like you better, for whatever that's worth. I'm sorry...things beyond our control got in the way."

As she departed, Tobias thought about the things he couldn't control. Then he acknowledged that women were able to control far less. However he'd felt about Lady Priscilla, or however she'd felt about him, it ultimately hadn't mattered.

Closing his eyes, he counted to twenty. Then fifty. When he reached one hundred, he went to the door and looked to make sure there was no one about before leaving the room.

Thirty minutes later, instead of racing north to Scotland, he walked into Brooks's and went directly to the Duke of Evesham's private chamber. The door stood slightly ajar, so he let himself in.

Once inside, he promptly poured himself a glass of the duke's secret Scotch whisky that had been smuggled south. The irony that Tobias had been about to smuggle a bride in the opposite direction nearly made him smile. Except he was still shaken by why he'd nearly done. Instead, he downed the contents and poured another.

"Bad night?" Lucien asked from the chair set closest to the hearth.

Tobias had registered his friend's presence but hadn't stopped to greet him. Lucien had, after all, invited him. "It did not go as planned. However, that is for the best."

Clutching his whisky, Tobias went to slump into a chair near Lucien, sprawling his legs out before him. He recounted his ill-conceived scheme and his thankful recollection of good sense.

Lucien winced before sipping his brandy. "I'll agree that it's best you abandoned your plan, but I am sorry for the way things worked out with Lady Priscilla."

"Unrequited love is unpleasant to say the least." Tobias frowned into his glass.

"My day has not been without news. My brother is marrying Lady Sabrina Kidd. Unlike you, I don't think this is a love situation at all. Con is simply doing his duty as demanded by our father. As usual." Lucien's lip curled before he took another drink.

"I was going to say congratulations to him, but perhaps I'll refrain. I'm not sure I can summon enthusiasm for anyone's marriage today." Tobias exhaled. "I suppose that makes me a selfish, maudlin ass."

Lucien's brow arched sharply. "Who am I to judge? The other news is that my father is giving up this room. I think this may be our last night here." He looked around the familiar, comfortable place until his gaze settled on a portrait of the duke that hung on the wall opposite the door. In it, Lucien's father was a young man. The duke stood with a horse, his expression painted with a mix of confidence and arrogance. While Tobias didn't always get along with his father, he was relieved not to be one of the duke's sons.

"That's bloody disappointing." Tobias sipped his whisky and stared at the bronze liquid for a moment. "I might miss this the most."

Lucien laughed. "I can get some."

"Brilliant. Actually, I'll miss the privacy and the ability to gather with my close friends." Tobias thought in particular about the day before, after the news of Lady Priscilla's betrothal had circulated. He'd come here and found a haven and solace.

"I feel the same, which has got me thinking. Perhaps it's time for a new place to gather."

"You have somewhere in mind?"

"I do, but it doesn't exist yet. I'm considering founding a club, one that is different from what we see along St. James. It wouldn't be just for men, to begin with."

Tobias sat up in his chair a bit and fixed his gaze on Lucien. "That is more than different. That's revolutionary." He wondered how it would work. Would women even join? Would men join knowing that women might be there? "What else?"

"This club will be incredibly exclusive." Lucien's eyes narrowed with purpose and perhaps a touch of dark mischief. "If people think White's is hard to access, they will be particularly frustrated by the entrance requirements for the Phoenix Club."

"The Phoenix Club?"

Lucien's lips spread in a sly grin. "A place to begin anew."

That sounded positively wonderful to Tobias, particularly in this moment. "This all sounds too good to be true. How will you manage it?"

"I've a location in mind, but it will take time to bring the physical location to fruition. In the meantime, I'm assembling our membership committee. As I said, it will be a most exclusive club."

Tobias let out a husky laugh. "How I would love to be on that committee."

"As it happens, I would be delighted if you would do so."

Having just sipped his whisky, Tobias nearly choked. After swallowing and coughing to clear his windpipe, he managed to say, "Hell, yes." He coughed again. "Who else are you asking?"

"I haven't entirely decided, but I do know there will be two secret members, and the identity of all members will be withheld from the public."

"I'll know the other members except for two?"

Lucien nodded. "Please don't ask me for their identity or why they will remain secret. Just know that the success of the club relies upon their participation and their anonymity."

"You sound as if you've plotted this quite thoroughly."

Lucien lifted his glass in a silent acknowledgment and took a drink.

"I look forward to hearing more when you are ready to share. Just tell me what I need to do."

"For now, recover from your broken heart." Lucien smirked, and Tobias rolled his eyes even as he felt a slight pang in his chest.

He wasn't angry or even disappointed in Lady Priscilla, but in himself. How he'd misjudged her feelings for him—rather, her absence of feelings for him—was what disappointed and angered him. The idea of the phoenix rose in his mind, making him eager to learn from this experience and emerge changed.

Love—and marriage—would be the furthest things from his mind. Which would infuriate his father. Tobias didn't care. The earl couldn't demand he wed.

Raising his glass, Tobias offered a toast. "To the Phoenix Club!"

Lucien inclined his head before lifting his whisky toward his lips. "To rebirth and a place we can call home."

# CHAPTER 5

*M*irabelle stared at the list she'd made of potential employment opportunities she could pursue. None of them were terribly exciting, but all of them were preferable to what she'd done the past four years. And she'd been luckier than most, starting her profession at a brothel that served the wealthy and well-positioned. From there, she'd transitioned almost immediately into becoming a courtesan, which had led her to a series of wealthy—and mostly kind—protectors, culminating in the best of them, Lord Lucien Westbrook.

Some would say she was foolish for terminating their arrangement and for refusing his assistance. Perhaps she was. She could not, however, continue the way that she was. In her future, she saw an endless stream of protectors, and she didn't want that. She didn't want to arrange her life around a man. She wanted freedom.

She did not, however, want poverty, and while she'd saved some funds, she would have to either live very frugally or find a way to provide for herself. Glancing down at the list once more, she tried to find even a breath of excitement for any of the things she'd written down.

"Miss Renault?" her housekeeper asked from the doorway of her sitting room. "Lord Lucien is here to see you. He said he's come to arrange your settlement."

Mirabelle wasn't sure what he meant by that. She'd been quite clear about not wanting him to take care of her. Frowning, she pushed her chair back from the desk and stood. "Show him in."

As she moved toward the small seating area in the center of the room, she smoothed her hand over the simple coral-colored gown she wore. She'd already decided to sell her more extravagant clothes and accessories since she'd no longer be attending Cyprian balls. The thought of parting with her finery made her throat clench. It was silly, but she loved her fashionable belongings, probably because in her youth, she'd had nothing of the kind. Instead, she'd seen her mother's maid making expensive gowns for other people. Was it wrong that Mirabelle wanted to look like she mattered?

As if clothes indicated one's import. Except in her experience, they absolutely did, along with education, upbringing, and, of course, one's origin and family. As a destitute French émigré and orphan, she was no one of consequence.

Lucien prowled into the sitting room, and immediately, the air shifted, as it always did. He was a force of masculine energy that commanded every space he entered, both due to his size and the sheer magnetism he exuded. Everyone who knew him liked him, and if they didn't know him, they wanted to. Actually, that wasn't true. There were some people who didn't care for him—he would list his father among them. Mirabelle categorized them all as idiots. And completely riddled with envy. That could be the only reason not to adore Lucien.

He bowed to her. "Good evening, Belle."

She stood in front of her chair, her hands clasped. "I don't know why you've come. I haven't changed my mind, nor will I."

"Then it's good that I don't wish for you to do so. I've come with a business proposition." He lowered himself to the settee and draped his arm along the back. "Will you sit?"

She wasn't sure if he meant for her to occupy the settee with him. In the past, she would have, snuggling up against his side and allowing her hand to rest on his thigh.

Tonight, she took the chair, perching on the edge amidst a burst of nervousness. Their relationship had changed, and she couldn't imagine what he meant to propose.

"You look incredibly dubious," Lucien said, sounding carefree. "Don't be. I promise I'm not going to suggest anything untoward. At least, I don't think it is." He took his arm from the back of the settee and leaned forward, resting his elbows on his knees and lightly clasping his hands between his legs. "What if you had the opportunity to be in charge of something, from its inception, but it would require you to completely change who you are?"

Mirabelle carefully considered his rather vague words. "Change how?"

"You couldn't be you anymore—a former courtesan named Mirabelle Renault. I'm afraid your name is too recognizable. Hopefully, your face won't be, but that will be something we'll address if the need arises."

She held up her hand. "Stop. You haven't fully explained yourself at all. What would I be in charge of?"

"I am starting a club, an exclusive establishment where

members, both men and women, will be specifically selected and invited to join."

Mirabelle's pulse quickened. "What sort of club?"

"I suppose it's like the gentlemen's clubs of St. James in that they are exclusive and provide a place to congregate with like souls. However, I prefer a club where the souls have more in common and are less...condescending."

Laughing, she tried to imagine what he was describing. "An exclusive club without arrogance? I find that hard to countenance. In fact, I imagine anything that comes from you would be hard-pressed to be devoid of conceit."

Sucking in a breath, Lucien straightened, touching his chest with one hand. "You wound me, Belle. Alas, I am aware of my shortcomings, most of them, anyway. I endeavor to find humility wherever I may. I trust you will always assist me in that endeavor."

"What an honor," she murmured.

He grinned as he sat back against the settee and crossed his legs. "I have always considered you a friend—a good one, in fact—and I hope you regard me in the same manner. I am also hopeful you will accept my offer of employment as manager of this new club."

Mirabelle was at a complete loss for words. After several moments, she swallowed as she tried to banish the sudden dryness from her mouth. "I haven't ever managed anything."

"Haven't you? You've told me how you helped your maid with her sewing projects and that you were always better at keeping track of things and organizing the funds. I've seen how you manage this household—you are far more economical than your peers."

She shook her head, her mind reeling. "That doesn't mean I'll be able to manage your club."

"What you don't know, you'll learn. You aren't really

going to say no, are you? Imagine yourself as an English widow who's come to London to manage this club because Society is not to your liking. You'll be an enigmatic figure people will crave to know."

To go from someone Society would never entertain to a person of import or popularity was nearly inconceivable. Mirabelle didn't need or want notoriety, just acceptance. "An English widow?"

"That's what I was thinking, unless you have a better idea?"

"No, that sounds as if it could be believable. To whom was I married?"

Lucien shrugged. "We'll invent some chap in…where would you like to have lived? You can't choose anywhere that doesn't sound like you. No Yorkshire unless you want to learn a new accent."

This sounded almost possible. Until someone uncovered her true identity. "What if someone recognizes me?"

"As I said, this club will be exclusive. No one is going to be admitted whom we don't personally select—and that includes you. You will serve on the membership committee."

"Me?" She could hardly believe any of this. "How would I know whom to choose?"

"We will start by searching for people who perhaps aren't accepted anywhere else, individuals who are looking for a new beginning, a second chance."

"People like me," she said softly. "Lucien, when did you think of starting this club?"

"Does it matter? It's already in motion. You can be a part of it or not, but I'd prefer you choose the former."

It was an excellent solution to what she should do next. Managing the club would be exciting and interesting, and she would be able to support herself. "I admit I do not know as much about Society as you, but how will a club that allows both men and women, and which is run by a woman, be seen as acceptable?"

"Because there will be two distinct sides: one for ladies and one for gentlemen. They will be kept separate, and the ladies' side will be overseen by a small but select group of respectable women, one of whom will be you."

She stared at him. "You've really thought this through. How can you be sure this group of women will accept me, a faux widow?"

"They won't know you're pretending, of course. And in the interest of establishing the truth as we wish it to be from the outset, please don't use those kinds of words. Just know that I have, indeed, thought this through. I have a very precise plan." He looked into her eyes. "Do you trust me?"

She shouldn't. And perhaps she didn't completely. "I trust you enough."

He laughed softly. "That's better than I expected, actually."

"Who are these other respectable women?"

"No one insufferable, I promise. They are not allowed."

"And who else is on the membership committee?" she asked.

"A few of my friends and a pair of people who will remain anonymous. Don't ask me who they are or why they will be unknown. Just know that I cannot start this club without them. They are wholly trustworthy, and they understand and support the spirit of the Phoenix Club."

"The *Phoenix* Club? I think it does matter to me when you conceived of this club, but I won't press you about it." Her gaze met his, and for the first time, the flutter she felt in her belly when she looked at him was not sexually charged. There was gratitude, respect, and friendship. "Thank you."

Lucien leaned forward again, his dark eyes sparkling. "Does that mean you're accepting the position?"

"Yes." They hadn't discussed wages, but that was one area in which she trusted him implicitly. If anything, he would probably try to pay her too much. "Where is the Phoenix Club to be located?"

"On Ryder Street, between Bury and Duke."

"So near to the St. James's clubs?"

"I liked the property." He lifted a shoulder, and the edge of his mouth ticked up. "And perhaps I appreciate the taunting nature of the proximity."

Mirabelle shook her head. "You would cock a snook at the entire ton if you could."

"I try every day. They deserve mockery—and that includes me." He slapped his palms on his thighs, then vaulted to his feet.

"I suppose you aren't rid of me, then." She looked up at him. "We will, however, just be friends."

"Yes." He went to her chair and took her hand. "I shall count myself very lucky to be your friend."

"And my boss," she added with a laugh.

"I fully expect you to be the boss, not me." He let go of her hand and straightened. "You must leave London for some months. Mirabelle Renault needs to disappear long before the English widow arrives. Where do you want to go?"

She thought for a moment. "I've always heard Cornwall is fair."

"It is quite lovely. Your employment includes a stipend while you are reinventing yourself." Mirabelle opened her mouth to object, but Lucien held up his hand. "That is nonnegotiable, I'm afraid. I think you must arrive in Bath in the fall, where you will make the necessary friends before they persuade you to come to London."

His plan really was precise. Overcome with appreciation, she merely nodded.

"Excellent. Enjoy your time away, Belle." He started to turn.

"Evangeline." The name tumbled from her lips the moment it entered her head. "Evangeline Renshaw."

Lucien pivoted and offered a bow. "Mrs. Renshaw, I'm delighted to make your acquaintance." His eyes sparkled with mischief before he turned and quit the room.

"You may call me Evie," Mirabelle murmured as she pressed her hands to her cheeks. Fortune had smiled upon her at last.

# CHAPTER 6

*March 1814*
*The Phoenix Club*
*Ryder Street, London*

"*I* don't think rake is a strong enough word. Wastrel is perhaps more fitting."

Lucien wiped his hand over his face, unable to dispute Evie's assessment of poor Tobias. His reputation had taken a hit the previous spring, and not because Lady Bentley, the former Lady Priscilla, had overlooked him in favor of her husband. It was because she'd told everyone that he'd wanted to kidnap her to Gretna Green. Her story concluded with her talking him out of it, but Lucien and their friends knew the truth.

Nevertheless, he'd become a pariah, and since Society thought him a rogue, he'd embraced their assumptions wholeheartedly. He'd spent the last several months drinking, gambling, and womanizing his way to the top of the list of London's Most Scandalous.

He lounged in his usual spot this evening, an oversized chair in the corner of the gaming room, a glass of some spirit dangling from his fingertips. Yes, wastrel was a more apt description. His father was horrified by his behavior, and the more he pressed upon Tobias to tidy himself up, the more deeply Tobias plunged into ignominy.

"He's fine," Ada Treadway, the club's bookkeeper, said quietly. She stood beside Evie, a delicate daisy next to Evie's brilliant, lush rose. They didn't spend a great deal of time on the gentlemen's side of the club, but on Tuesdays, this side welcomed women into their members' den.

Evie snapped her head toward Ada. "You don't have a tendre for our resident profligate, do you?"

A light tremor passed over Ada's shoulders. "No. I simply like him. I like everyone."

Lucien smiled warmly. "Indeed you do, which is a lovely trait." Evie had brought Ada back to London with her. Lucien did not know the entire story of what had brought her here, other than she'd been a governess and decided that work didn't suit her. She'd needed to begin anew, and there was no better place for that than the Phoenix Club.

"I'll go and speak with him," Ada said. "He really just needs a friend." She took herself off toward Tobias.

Lucien looked about the gaming room, where several members played cards and others billiards. He turned to Evie. "Is everything ready for our first ball next week?"

When they'd designed the renovations that had split this one house into the two distinct parts of the Phoenix Club, he'd come up with the idea to have a removable partition on the ground floor that would allow them to open up a large ballroom between the two sides. On

Fridays, they would host a ball, which would be the only time young, unwed ladies on the Marriage Mart could enter the club. They were still not members, of course, but they could attend a ball with a sponsor who was a member.

"Yes. I'm rather nervous about it. If the food and drink is not regarded as superior to Almack's, I will consider it a failure."

He chuckled. "As will I. But rest assured, that will not be difficult to achieve."

Evie put her hand on his arm, and they walked through the parlor to the stair hall. As they entered, he heard a commotion from the next room, the entrance hall.

Glancing at Evie, whose expression had grown concerned, he took her hand from his arm and said, "Wait here."

Lucien stalked into the entrance hall as a gentleman's voice rose. "I'm a new member. You must let me in!" He tried to push past the two footmen who were barring his entrance into the club.

"Someone trying to force their way in?" Lucien asked from behind his employees.

"Yes, my lord." One footman moved to the side, which allowed Lucien to see the nuisance.

"Good evening, Bentley." Lucien stepped up to the threshold. The footmen had done an excellent job of keeping the man outside. "Did I hear you say you're a new member?"

Bentley, a large man but with little athletic prowess, given his extreme struggle and subsequent failure in trying to push past the two footmen, scowled, for he knew Lucien owned the club—everyone did. "I should be. Where is my invitation?"

"Nonexistent. And let me tell you, this is not the manner in which you go about trying to obtain one."

Lucien didn't remotely try to keep the glee from his voice.

"This is because of Deane. Your support of him is pathetic. Cut him loose, and you'll find your invitations will improve." Damp strands of Bentley's brown hair fell over his forehead. He attempted to brush it back into some semblance of style, but failed rather spectacularly as it flopped forward once more.

"My invitations are just fine. It seems yours are the ones which are lacking." Lucien gave the man a pitying stare. "Now, if you can't behave like a gentleman and leave of your own accord, my men will see that you're removed. Please don't make them work harder than they ought."

Pivoting on his heel, Lucien found Evie standing in the center of the entrance hall with a satisfied smile playing about her lips. She clapped her hands. "Well done."

He bowed. "Thank you. Just a minor irritation."

"I do wish people would stop trying to force their way in." Evie shook her head as they turned together to return to the stair hall.

This was the second time this week someone had sought to gain entrance by claiming membership. The employees of the club were well trained as to who was a member and who was not. "Do you truly?" Lucien asked. "I admit I find their desperation somewhat satisfying."

She gently swatted his arm. "You're terrible."

"What, you don't agree?"

A smile crept over her dark pink lips. "I don't *dis*agree. It serves some people right to feel excluded."

"Precisely." He'd wanted to create a place where those who were often and usually excluded, derided, or completely cast out were able to feel welcome and wanted. Those who didn't belong could suffer the consequences of being haughty, condescending prigs.

Lucien offered Evie his arm as they ascended the stairs. The first floor contained the primary rooms of the club: the drawing room that overlooked the corner of Ryder and Bury Streets and the largest chamber in the club, which Lucien had dubbed the members' den.

As they entered the members' den, Lucien inclined his head toward a trio of middle-aged ladies seated at a table, proof positive that welcoming the club's ladies to the gentlemen's side one night each week was something people wanted. One was the widow of a disgraced gentleman who'd died of an apoplectic attack in a rather compromising position in a brothel. Another was a never-married woman —a spinster—and the sister of the third woman, a lady who had married a baron fifteen years her junior. He was glad they had a place to gather, where they could enjoy being out and connecting with people who wouldn't judge them. If he did nothing else, this would be enough.

"You look happy," Evie murmured.

He glanced at her, marveling at how different she looked now. Along with changing her name, she'd changed her style. She only wore gray, silver, or purple in the latest, most conservative style, and her dark hair, due to some sort of powder, now appeared a shade lighter. "It's going well, don't you think?"

"I do. I only wish my sister could come to see it."

"She will—someday. They have already accepted their invitations to join the club. Has the babe arrived yet?" Lucien asked. Heloise and her husband were expecting a child any time.

"Not that I've heard, but the mail takes a few days. I could be an aunt already."

He heard the tremor of emotion in her voice. "You are welcome to take time to go and see them. Should I insist?"

Evie squeezed his arm. "I'll go in the summer. By then, Ada will be able to run things in my absence."

"Are you ever going to tell me the specifics of how you made her acquaintance?"

"Here comes Ruark. I'll let you speak with him." She withdrew her hand from Lucien's arm.

Lucien narrowed his eyes at her. "If I didn't know better, I'd say you orchestrated that to avoid answering my question."

Her dark brows arched as she gave him a look of mock innocence before gliding away.

Smiling to himself, Lucien turned to greet Ruark.

"Evening, Lucien," Ruark said, briefly clasping his hand. "I wonder if I might borrow you for a ...matter?"

"A matter? That sounds potentially serious."

Ruark flashed a bright smile. "Probably not."

Lucien noted his use of the word probably. "How can I help?"

"I want to introduce you to a friend. Is there somewhere we can talk privately?"

Lucien had an office and private sitting room on the second floor. "Certainly. Let's go upstairs. Where is your friend?"

"A moment." Ruark went to the corner where a gentleman sat in a chair near one of the doors that led out to the veranda that overlooked the garden, which was still being finished. When they returned, Lucien recognized the fellow. Because he knew everyone who belonged to his club.

"Good evening, Lawler," Lucien said as he gestured for them to accompany him from the members' den. He led them up the stairs to his private office, which sat directly above the also private selection chamber where the

membership committee met fortnightly to discuss potential members and voted to extend invitations.

Lucien's sitting room smelled of fresh paint and wood,
having just been finished several days ago. Bookcases lined
two walls, while a hearth occupied the third, and windows
facing the garden marked the fourth.

"Please, sit." Lucien gestured to the seating area as he
took a chair.

"I'll let you talk," Ruark said. He gave Lawler a mean-
ingful look before turning and leaving, closing the door
behind him.

Lawler shifted nervously before perching on the edge
of a chair. "Thank you for seeing me, my lord."

"Wexford mentioned you have a…matter."

"Yes. It's, ah, rather delicate."

"You think I can help?"

Lawler nodded, his wide blue eyes glossy with hope.
"My valet has a sister who works as a maid in a…prom-
inent Mayfair household. She is uncomfortable in her
current position because of inappropriate behavior by a
member of the household."

"I take it this is not another servant exhibiting the
behavior?"

"No." Lawler's shoulders relaxed, and he exhaled. "I'm
glad you understand."

"Not entirely, but I can imagine. Can this maid leave
her employment?"

Lawler shook his head. "My valet says she cannot. I
understand some of the people who work here are those
who needed help…" He let his question hang in the air. At
least, Lucien believed there was a question there.

"You'd like me to offer this maid a job?"

"Or perhaps help her find one? I thought you might do
that too."

He had, in fact. He'd given jobs at the club to people in need of employment and lodgings. The lived on the upper-most floor. In one case, he'd secured a position for a woman who did not want to work there. She was quite happy now as a clerk in Cheapside. "How did you hear I would do that?" he asked Lawler.

"People talk."

"Which people?" Lucien wanted to know how this information was getting out—not because he cared that people knew what he'd done. On the contrary, if he could help someone, he would do so.

Rubbing his palms along his thighs, Lawler looked as if a bit of his anxiety was returning. "I can't rightly recall."

"It's all right, Lawler, I'd be happy to help this maid." Just as he'd been eager to invite Lawler to join the club. With an overbearing father, and a dearth of confidence, Lawler was in need of a boost. Lucien hoped the club would provide the young man with an opportunity to build his strength and character in a place where he would feel welcome and included. "Will you have her come see me when she next has time off?"

Lawler's face brightened. "Of course. Thank you, my lord. You are incredibly kind. Not at all the devil I've heard you called."

Lucien had begun to hear that moniker as well. He chuckled. "Perhaps it's meant in fun instead of as an insult." In all likelihood, it was borne of envy because he wouldn't invite everyone to join his club. If that were the case, he'd embrace the description wholeheartedly.

"Thank you for approaching me about this," Lucien said. Perhaps the club was already having a positive effect on the lad.

Lawler stood. "Thank *you*. Truly. The invitation to join

this club has been the greatest thing that ever happened to me."

"I daresay what you've just done to help someone else might end up being even greater." Lucien went to open the door. "Now, go and enjoy some port."

As Lucien watched Lawler turn the corner to go back downstairs, Evie emerged from the shadows of the antechamber outside his sitting room.

"What did you do?" she asked with a half smile.

"Nothing we haven't already."

"We're going to be known for fixing things," she said, moving into his sitting room. "On second thought, you will be known for that. I can't effect even a fraction of what you can do. At least not without your help."

"Not true. You've become a woman of power in your own right. Surely you can see that."

"Perhaps there's a glimpse. Time will tell." She sat down and leaned against the tall back of the chair. "Pour me a brandy, please?"

"Yes, and then you can tell me how we might employ a young maid in need of a job."

∽

*January, 1815*

The familiar smell of the Phoenix Club, of pine and some spice he couldn't name—a scent Lucien had commissioned and used to give the place a distinctive air, lifted Tobias's sagging spirits as he stepped into the entrance hall.

"Good afternoon, Lord Overton," the footman said

crisply, taking Tobias's hat and gloves. And using his new title.

"Thank you, Dexter. I trust Lord Lucien is in his office at this hour?"

Dexter inclined his prematurely gray head. The footmen at the Phoenix Club did not wear wigs as they did in so many others. "Indeed he is."

Tobias thanked him again before going up to the second floor to Lucien's office. The door to his outer sitting room was open, so Tobias strode inside only to stop short at seeing Lucien in quiet conversation with a young just outside his open office door.

Lucien's gaze lifted as he looked over the woman's shoulder and acknowledged Tobias. "I'll see you soon," he said to her.

She turned, and, keeping her head down, darted by Tobias on her way out.

"I'm sorry to interrupt," Tobias said, thinking the woman seemed in an exceptional hurry to leave—and not be noticed by Tobias. "Helping another soul in need?"

"Yes." Lucien beckoned him to his office.

"Good, then you're already in the mood."

Lucien closed the door and arched a brow at Tobias. "You need help?"

"So much." Tobias dropped into a chair. "My father has left me...a mess."

"Brandy?" Lucien offered.

Tobias nodded.

Moving to pour their drinks, Lucien said, "I would have thought your father would have left things in an exceedingly orderly manner."

"Orderly for him, yes. For me?" Tobias shook his head, the familiar frustration and anger he'd felt since his father's death swelling in his chest. "He had a ward."

"That is a surprise." Lucien handed him a glass and sat in a nearby chair. "Is that why you need help?"

"She'll be here in a fortnight for her Season. I'm to keep my father's promise to her father and see her wed. She will need a chaperone and a sponsor. I have neither, nor do I know how to obtain them." He pinned Lucien with a desperate stare. "Who is going to sponsor a ward of *mine*?"

Lucien's lips spread into an easy smile. "Leave that to me. I've just the lady in mind. And, as it happens, I have the perfect chaperone and lady's companion. You just encountered her, in fact."

Tobias glanced toward the door. "The woman who practically ran away when I arrived?"

"I promise she is more than equal to the task. When have I ever led you astray?"

Tobias thought about that. While Lucien had been, as was his nature, an always helpful participant in Tobias's debauchery over the past two years, he hadn't led him anywhere Tobias hadn't tried to go first.

Taking a long drink, Tobias let the heat of the brandy calm him. It had been a trying month since his father's death, and the news that he now had a ward wasn't even the worst of it.

"There's something else," Lucien said softly. "Is it about this ward?"

Tobias shook his head. "No, it's about me. If I don't wed within three months of my father's death, I will forfeit my mother's holdings." The thought of losing her house in Wiltshire, the very center of every bit of happiness in his youth, stole his breath. His father was far more cruel than Tobias had ever imagined. That, or he had no idea how much the house meant to Tobias. Either way, Tobias felt as though he hadn't known the man at all.

"I'm so sorry." Lucien's brow creased as he regarded

him over his raised glass. "I suppose your father has the last word when it comes to his demands that you wed."

"So it seems," Tobias muttered. He took another drink before looking resolutely to his friend. "You can wave your magic wand and present me with a chaperone and a sponsor. Any chance you can find me a tolerable wife?"

**Don't miss the first full-length novel in THE PHOENIX CLUB, IMPROPER! Read on for a sneak peek at chapter one!**

**Find out what happens when a dissolute guardian (that's Tobias!) must rehabilitate his reputation to launch his very proper young ward in Society only to discover she's a hellion in disguise...**

Would you like to know when my next book is available and to hear about sales and deals? Sign up for my VIP newsletter, follow me on social media:

Facebook: https://facebook.com/DarcyBurkeFans
Twitter at @darcyburke
Instagram at darcyburkeauthor
Pinterest at darcyburkewrite

And follow me on Bookbub to receive updates on pre-orders, new releases, and deals!

**Need more Regency romance? Check out my other historical series:**

**The Untouchables**
Swoon over twelve of Society's most eligible and elusive

bachelor peers and the bluestockings, wallflowers, and outcasts who bring them to their knees!

### The Untouchables: The Spitfire Society

Meet the smart, independent women who've decided they don't need Society's rules, their families' expectations, or, most importantly, a husband. But just because they don't need a man doesn't mean they might not *want* one...

### The Untouchables: The Pretenders

Set in the captivating world of The Untouchables, follow the saga of a trio of siblings who excel at being something they're not. Can a dauntless Bow Street Runner, a devastated viscount, and a disillusioned Society miss unravel their secrets?

### Wicked Dukes Club

Six books written by me and my BFF, NYT Bestselling Author Erica Ridley. Meet the unforgettable men of London's most notorious tavern, The Wicked Duke. Seductively handsome, with charm and wit to spare, one night with these rakes and rogues will never be enough...

### Love is All Around

Heartwarming Regency-set retellings of classic Christmas stories (written after the Regency!) featuring a cozy village, three siblings, and the best gift of all: love.

### Secrets and Scandals

Six epic stories set in London's glittering ballrooms and England's lush countryside.

### Legendary Rogues

Five intrepid heroines and adventurous heroes embark on

exciting quests across the Georgian Highlands and
Regency England and Wales!

If you like contemporary romance, I hope you'll check out
my **Ribbon Ridge** series available from Avon Impulse, and
the continuation of Ribbon Ridge in **So Hot**.

I hope you'll consider leaving a review at your favorite
online vendor or networking site!

I appreciate my readers so much. Thank you, thank you,
*thank you.*

# IMPROPER

## CHAPTER ONE

*London, February, 1815*

Tobias Powell, fifth Earl of Overton, smiled faintly at the brush of his mistress's fingertips along his shoulder. He didn't open his eyes and instead pressed himself into the bedclothes, as if he could hug the cozy softness of the bed. He was particularly tired today, but then it had been a viciously late night.

"What time is your ward arriving?" Barbara, his soon-to-be-former mistress asked from behind him.

*Bloody hell, his ward.* His eyes shot open as he pushed himself to a sitting position, the bedclothes falling away from his nude body. "What time is it?"

"Three."

"In the afternoon?" Of course in the afternoon. They hadn't even come back to Barbara's lodgings until the sun was rising over London.

Tobias scrambled from the bed and ran about plucking up his carelessly tossed clothing. Foregoing the small-clothes since he couldn't seem to find them, he pulled his breeches on. He threw his shirt over his head and haphazardly tucked the ends into his waistband.

From the bed, Barbara held up the missing smallclothes, her wide, red lips parting in a teasing smile. "Don't you need these?"

"You kept those from me on purpose."

She shrugged, her elegant shoulders arching, which made her rather large breasts also move.

Tobias groaned. "I have to go. My ward could already have arrived." This was not how he'd intended things to happen. He was supposed to be on his best, non-scandalous behavior, both to support his ward's debut and to find his own wife. "You are far too tempting, Barbara." He narrowed his eyes at her as he tugged his waistcoat on.

"Your buttons are not aligned." She laughed softly as she leaned back against the head of the bed, making no attempt to cover her exposed upper half.

Tobias looked down and saw that she was right. Cursing softly, he started over. "This is your fault. You're a terrible distraction."

She stretched one arm up over her head, which again accentuated her breasts. "You like me that way."

"I like you every way, but you know this is our final meeting. It has to be."

Lowering her arm, she at last pulled up the bedclothes to cover her chest. Pouting, she said, "Because you must marry. *Immediately.*"

Flinging himself in a chair, Tobias began to don his stockings and boots. "Within the next five or so weeks, yes." Because his father had decreed it in a surprising change to his will before he'd died in December.

Tobias had to wed within three months of the former earl's death or he'd lose the property that as not entailed— Tobias's mother's house, the location of every single one of his happy memories. He would do anything to keep it in his possession. Which meant he had to find a wife with nearly impossible haste.

And it was only *nearly* impossible because of his own behavior the past two years. While there were many who would gleefully accept an earl's suit, he didn't want just anyone. He wanted a wife of sophistication and wit, one who was kind and caring.

Someone he could love, even if he didn't at the outset. Because he had no bloody time to fall in love. He needed to find a suitable woman, settle the betrothal, have the banns read, and complete the marriage ceremony within five weeks. All while any woman worth having would likely turn her back to him.

Reformation was the plan, and so far he was not following it. He'd tried to break things off with Barbara the other day, but he'd encountered her last night, and she'd been incredibly persuasive.

Finishing with his boots, he stood and drew on his coat. His cravat was also lost apparently. No matter, it would have been a horribly wrinkled mess. He grabbed his hat and gloves from the top of her dresser and went to the bed.

"This really was the last time, Barb. You know it has to be."

She exhaled, her dark eyes meeting his with a shadow of sadness. "I'll find someone else, but they won't be you. They'll be serious and boring, and they won't know me at all."

Tobias brushed a dark blonde lock from her cheek and bent to press a kiss to her temple. "They'll come to know you, and you'll cure them of their dullness." He straightened and set his hat atop his head.

"Perhaps I'll take your generous settlement and just wait for you to change your mind." She smiled up at him, and Tobias suffered a moment's regret. He didn't love Barbara, but she made him feel good and that was a lovely thing.

He turned and left her rooms then practically sprinted down to the street where he hailed a hack. Three in the afternoon! He really hoped his ward had not yet arrived. It was a long journey from Shropshire, and the winter weather could have delayed her. Yes, he'd hope that was the case. Hadn't that been one of the arguments Barbara had used the night before to persuade him to go home with her? She'd cooed that his ward was likely stuck somewhere due to a washed out road.

Not that it had taken much to sway him. He'd fallen eagerly and completely into debauchery without a shred of regret. That his behavior would have frustrated his father —and did while he was alive—only made it more attractive. After Tobias had failed to wed two years ago, his father had harassed him incessantly about taking a wife. Hence, his dying decree that Tobias marry or suffer—by taking the one possession that meant something incredibly dear to him.

And so his father would win, as if this had been a game the past two years. It hadn't, not to Tobias. He thought he'd fallen in love, only to have the lady in question turn on him and make him doubt everything he'd felt. Was it any wonder he was not inclined to court anyone else?

It was, however, time he did.

The hack stopped halfway down Brook Street, and Tobias leapt from the vehicle. He dashed through the gate and up the steps to his house, rushing inside as Carrin opened the door.

He stopped abruptly, facing the butler. "Is she here?"

"Miss Wingate?" Carrin shook his head. "Not yet, my lord."

The stress rushed out Tobias's frame, making him feel as if he might slide down to the marble floor. "Thank God. I'm going to take a quick bath." He removed his hat and strode through the archway into the staircase hall.

"I believe she's just arrived, my lord," Carrin called just as Tobias put his foot on the stair.

Closing his eyes, he gripped the railing. "Bollocks."

"Oh my goodness, that's Hyde Park!" Fiona Wingate pressed her nose to the window of the coach, her pulse racing.

"How do you know?" Mrs. Tucket said without opening her eyes from beside Fiona.

"Because I do." Fiona had studied maps of London for as long as she could remember. Indeed, she'd studied maps of everywhere. "It's so big and wonderful." She splayed her gloved palm against the glass as if she could somehow reach through and touch the trees, their spindly limbs still bare.

Mrs. Tucket leaned against her, and a quick look showed she'd opened one eye long enough to peer past Fiona at the park. "Harumph. You can't see anything of import."

No, she couldn't see Rotten Row or the Serpentine or any of the ton's ladies and gentlemen who would be out and about during the fashionable hour. She doubted they'd be out today anyway. It was quite early in the Season, with Parliament just starting their session a few days earlier. And it was certainly too cold to promenade.

At that moment, rain drops splattered the window. Certainly too rainy.

Fiona didn't care. She'd take London in the rain, the

snow, even in a hurricane, if such a thing were possible. The point was, she didn't care about the weather or that the park was not yet in full bloom. She was in *London*. Most importantly, she was no longer in Bitterley, where she'd spent the entirety of her almost twenty-two years.

Mrs. Tucket exhaled loudly as she worked to push herself into an upright sitting position. She'd slumped rather far down in her seat since their last stop some miles back. "I suppose I must rouse myself from the travel stupor."

Fiona kept her face to the window until they reached the corner of the park. Even then, she craned her neck to look back at it, marveling at the archway leading inside. She would get to promenade there or mayhap even ride. Perhaps her guardian would drive her in his phaeton. If he had one. But surely all earls had phaetons.

The coach continued along a bustling street—Oxford Street, if she recalled the map correctly, and she was certain she did. Shortly they would turn right down Davies Street into the heart of London's most fashionable neighborhood, Mayfair.

They passed stone and brick faced houses, some with elaborate doorways and others with wide windows. Some were narrow while others were twice as wide. When they turned left onto Brook Street, the houses became quite elegant with fancy wrought iron fencing and pillared entrances.

At last, the coach drew to a halt in front of the most glorious house yet. An iron gate with a large O worked into the design at the top guarded the walkway leading to the front door where a pair of pillars stood on either side. The door of the coach opened, and a footman dressed in dark green livery rushed through the gate to help her descend.

Fiona tipped her head back and counted four storeys stretching into the gray sky. A raindrop landed on her nose, and she grinned. Then she glanced down at the part of the house below the street. Five storeys in all.

"I think my legs have completely gone to sleep," Mrs. Tucket said, grasping Fiona's arm to steady herself.

The footman held the gate open and indicated Fiona and Mrs. Tucket should precede him. Holding her head high, Fiona made sure Mrs. Tucket had a good hold on her before moving through the gate onto the short path that took them to five steps. Fiona went slowly so Mrs. Tucket, who had an aching hip, could keep up. This was more than fine since Fiona's heart was beating even faster than it had been in the coach as she contemplated the ways in which her life was about to change.

She was the ward of an earl in London on the brink of her first Season. It was, in a word, unbelievable.

The door stood open and another man in dark green livery was positioned just inside. "Good afternoon, Miss Wingate, Mrs. Tucket. Welcome to Overton House."

"You've arrived!" The booming masculine voice sounded through the marble-floored, wood-paneled foyer before Fiona could see the man himself. But then he, presumably the Earl of Overton, was there, striding through a wide archway directly across from them.

Fiona stared at him, surprised at his youth. No, not his youth, for he was likely almost thirty. No, she was surprised to see that he was...handsome. She'd expected someone like his father, whom she'd met a dozen or so times over the course of her lifetime. But where the former earl had been dour-faced and without any exceptional physical traits, the current earl possessed a lively gaze, his eyes the color of pewter. His dark hair was damp; artful waves contrasting against his light forehead. He tugged at his coat and fidgeted with his simply-knotted cravat as he came to stand in the center of the foyer.

Recalling her practice with Mrs. Tucket, Fiona sank into a deep curtsey while her arm was still in her maid's grasp. "My lord."

"Well done," he said, grinning. "You are nearly ready for your presentation to the queen."

Fiona had started to rise but she nearly toppled to the floor. "My what?"

"You're to be presented to the queen?" Mrs. Tucket began to breathe heavily, so much so that Fiona feared she would faint.

"Can she sit?" Fiona asked, searching wildly for a chair.

Lord Overton's brow creased as he hurried forward to take Mrs. Tucket's other arm. "In here." He ushered them to a sitting room to the right of the foyer. Decorated in warm yellow and burnished bronze, the room welcomed them like a sunny afternoon.

Together, Fiona and the earl brought Mrs. Tucket to a chair near the hearth where coals burned in the fireplace. "Better?" Fiona asked.

"A drop of sherry would not come amiss," Mrs. Tucket said, untying her bonnet beneath her chin.

The earl stalked back to the doorway and asked someone to fetch sherry and tea. "Carrin will be along presently. That's the butler. He was standing just in the foyer when you arrived. I'll introduce you to the household a bit later, if that's all right."

"Yes, thank you," Fiona said, trying not to gape at the splendor of the room with its multiple paintings, rich window hangings, and lavish furniture. She'd known the earl would have a large house and fine décor, but she hadn't realized how large or how fine. And now it was her *home*. Her heart started to pound again.

Mrs. Tucket coughed. "Were you jesting about my Fiona being presented to the queen? Surely you must have been."

"Not at all," Overton said with a smile. "It is expected that young ladies entering upon their first Season are presented to Her Royal Highness."

Now it felt as if Fiona's heart might actually leap from her chest. The queen!

Mrs. Tucket's dark eyes widened, and she stared at Fiona in something akin to horror, which was just a wee bit annoying. "She doesn't know a thing about how to do that!"

The earl continued to smile placidly. "Do not fret, for Miss Wingate shall have ample opportunity to prepare. Her presentation is not until next week."

"Next week?" Mrs. Tucket squeaked as she drooped in the chair. She pressed the back of her hand to her cheek and muttered something unintelligible.

Moving to stand near Fiona, the earl murmured, "Er, is she all right?"

"Yes, she's just being dramatic," Fiona whispered. "She does that."

"Oh. Then I daresay it's wise that I've procured a chaperone and a sponsor for you. You'll meet the former shortly and the latter tomorrow."

"Did I hear you say you've hired a chaperone for my Fiona?" Mrs. Tucket sounded aghast. She pursed her lips most strenuously. "*I* am her chaperone."

The earl smiled affably. "Certainly, but I thought she might benefit from an additional chaperone, someone acquainted with London and Society." He darted an uncertain look at Fiona, as if he were looking for support.

"An excellent idea, my lord," Fiona said as she went to sit in another chair near the hearth. She reached over and patted Mrs. Tucket's hand. "How can I not prosper with two chaperones?"

"Harumph." Mrs. Tucket narrowed her eyes at the fire.

Fiona looked up at the earl. He was frowning, one hand on his hip and the other stroking his chin.

The butler arrived with a tray bearing tea and a glass of sherry. The earl scooped up the latter item and brought it directly to Mrs. Tucket. "Your sherry, ma'am."

She took the glass and downed half the contents without a word. Holding the sherry against her chest, she settled back against the chair and closed her eyes.

Fiona slowly rose and tiptoed back to the center of the room where the earl stood staring at her maid. "She'll likely fall asleep in a moment. The key will be to catch the glass before it falls."

The earl's dark brows climbed just before he nodded. Turning, he gestured for the butler to move the tray to a table in front of the windows that looked out to Brook Street.

A snore rattled the air, and Fiona dashed to catch the glass of sherry as Mrs. Tucket's grip slackened. Just one small drop of the contents splashed over the side onto her skirt. Fiona considered that a victory.

When she joined the earl at the table near the window, he inclined his head with appreciation. "Well done."

"It is not my first rescue."

The earl held her chair as she sat. "I see, and here I thought you had someone taking care of you."

"She does take care of me, but it's true that I also take care of her. More in the last year or so. She's quite tired, I think. She all but ran our household the past six years after my father died and then later when my mother became ill."

The earl, seated across the round table, handed her a cup of tea, which the butler had prepared before leaving.

The entire activity—the delivery of the tea, organizing it and a selection of food on the table, and his departure had occurred with such ease and precision that Fiona wondered how the butler had done it, all without her really noticing.

"How long since she's been gone?" Overton asked before sipping his tea.

"Not quite two years. She'd hoped to come to London with me for my Season, but, ah, your father, didn't extend the invitation until just before she died. And then, well…" She didn't need to tell him about how things had happened. "I didn't mean to imply anything by that."

"Of course not," he said benignly, reaching for a biscuit. "You need never fear voicing an opinion about my father. You'll find I have many, and few of them are good."

"Oh." Fiona didn't know what to say to that, so she decided to find another topic. It wasn't hard, for she had a thousand questions. And that was before she'd learned she was to be presented to the queen or that she would have a new chaperone and a…sponsor? "What does a sponsor do?"

He finished chewing and waved his hand, still holding the biscuit. "An excellent question. You are quite fortunate to be sponsored by one of Society's most influential ladies, Lady Pickering." He waggled his brows. "She will come tomorrow, and you'll discuss all things of import, including your presentation to court, your wardrobe, and, of course, invitations."

Fiona had just picked up a biscuit and promptly dropped it into her teacup. "I already have invitations?"

"Not yet. No one knows who you are, and the Season has barely begun. Lady Pickering will see that you receive invitations. Once you're presented, there will likely be a flood."

Fiona picked up her teacup and frowned into the contents where the edge of the biscuit was visible just above the liquid.

"Let's just pour you a new cup." He reached for the third cup that was likely for Mrs. Tucket, who wouldn't be needing it. After pouring the tea, he added a bit of milk and sugar then swapped it with her cup with an efficiency and care she would not have expected from an earl.

She couldn't help but smile at him. "You're quite jovial." She didn't recall his father being so likeable. He'd been rather serious.

"I try to be." He finished the rest of his biscuit while Fiona sampled her new cup of tea.

"Better?" he asked.

"Much, thank you." She set her cup down just as he picked his up.

"THE BLOODY QUEEN?"

The outburst from Mrs. Tucket caused the earl to spill his tea right down the front of his cravat and waistcoat. His eyes, wide with shock, darted toward Mrs. Tucket, still slumped in her chair. "Is she all right?"

"Oh, yes. She does that." Fiona picked up her napkin and went to the earl, dabbing at the tea on his front without thinking.

"Er." His gaze met hers—they were rather close—and Fiona realized this was highly improper.

"Sorry!" She dropped the now-soiled napkin in his lap and dashed back to her chair, heat rushing up her neck and cheeks.

He plucked the napkin up and continued where she left off. "It's fine. I appreciate your quick reaction. Mrs. Tucket often shouts in her sleep?" He looked toward her again, one brow arching. "She *is* still asleep?"

"Most certainly. At this time of day, she typically naps

an hour or two. And, yes, she is known to call out. Usually with a profanity."

His hand stopped wiping at his waistcoat as his gaze fixed on her. "Truly?" At her answering nod, he let out a wonderfully warm laugh. Fiona couldn't help but join in.

When their laughter subsided, he set the napkin on the edge of the table. "Well, it's good that I've enlisted additional help. You will require a chaperone who does not fall asleep and make exclamations using inappropriate language."

Fiona leaned forward slightly. "You can't dismiss her. I won't allow it."

The earl studied her in silent a moment. "I'm afraid it's not up to you to allow things," he said with a subtle edge of steel. "However, it was never my plan to dismiss her. I understand she's been with your family quite some time. She will simply take on a new role."

His plan. It wasn't up to her. Perhaps Overton wasn't as likeable as she thought. "Thank you, my lord," she said as sweetly as possible. "What role is that?"

"Whatever you deem it to be. Just know she will not accompany you to Society events. That will be Miss Lancaster's responsibility."

"Miss Lancaster?"

He stood. "Come, I'll introduce you now." Looking toward Mrs. Tucket, he pressed his lips together. "Should we wake her? I can have Mrs. Smythe, the housekeeper, see her upstairs."

Fiona went to assess Mrs. Tucket's situation. She didn't look particularly comfortable, but Fiona knew that didn't matter. What did matter was not interrupting this most important afternoon nap, particularly after their long, arduous journey over the past week. "She'll sleep another hour at least. Would it be possible to have a maid check on her periodically so she doesn't startle when she awakens? She may not recall where she is."

The earl looked alarmed. "She's forgetful?"

"Occasionally, but so is anyone nearing seventy. This is a new place and we've only just arrived. I fear *I* might not recall where I was."

"Fair enough." He gestured to the door. "Shall we?"

The tea had stained the folds of his cravat, and parts of his maroon waistcoat were darker than the rest because the fabric was wet. She would feel bad if his clothing were ruined, but then he could surely afford to replace both items without a second thought.

He led her from the sitting room back into the foyer. A liveried footman stood near the door like a statue. They turned to the right, and there was an actual statue in the corner, a life-sized rendering of a muscular young man in a brimmed hat, winged sandals, and a cloth draped in an artful fashion, covering his most intimate parts.

"Is that Hermes?" she asked.

"You know your Greek gods." He sounded impressed. "My father liked Greek mythology in his youth. Or so my mother said."

He led her into a large hall in which a wide staircase climbed up the right side. Portraits lined the wall ascending to the first floor.

"I seem to recall that about him when he visited my father. They discussed Greek philosophers too." She looked at the paintings as they went up. "Are these your relatives?"

"Yes." He pointed to the one at the top. "That's my grandmother. She lives at the dowager house at Deane Hall. She rarely comes to London anymore."

The likeness was of a woman past the blush of youth, but not yet in middle age. Her gray-blue eyes were very similar to that of her grandson, including a certain sense of exuberance, as if she were ready to meet whatever came her way. "She looks lively."

"She has many opinions and will share them whether you want to hear them or not." At the top of the stairs, he continued onto the next flight. "Your room is up one more."

The staircase up to the second floor was not quite as grand, and the paintings were of landscapes. There was also one of a bowl of fruit.

"Just to the left here." He led her to a doorway and stepped into a small, well-appointed sitting room decorated in pale pink and green. Once inside, he gestured to the right. "Your chamber is through there. And here is Miss Lancaster."

The woman who was to be Fiona's companion walked into the sitting room from a door on the wall opposite the one to Fiona's chamber. Miss Lancaster was taller than average with dark blonde hair and a narrow face. Her pale, gray-green eyes were wide, however, and fringed with long, dark lashes. There was a steel to her, perhaps in the way she stood or the manner in which she held her head, with an air of resolve.

Fiona moved toward her with a warm smile, wanting to start their relationship off well, even if she did feel a bit like the woman was edging Mrs. Tucket out. "Good afternoon, I'm pleased to make your acquaintance."

Miss Lancaster dropped into a gentle curtsey. "I have been eager to meet you, Miss Wingate. And to be of service."

"I will let the two of you become acquainted," the earl said. "Dinner is at eight."

"So late?" Fiona asked. "Mrs. Tucket will be quite famished by then, I should think."

"We don't keep country hours here in town," Overton said. "But we'll do our best to accommodate Mrs. Tucket. I'll see she has whatever refreshments she desires. As soon as she wakes," he added.

"Where is her room?" Fiona glanced toward the door from which Miss Lancaster had emerged.

"Across the gallery overlooking Brook Street. I'm sure she'll find it more than acceptable. See you at dinner." He turned and left before Fiona could ask any more questions.

Instead, she addressed Miss Lancaster. "Is that your room there then?" Fiona inclined her head toward the door that didn't lead to Fiona's chamber.

"Yes. His lordship thought we should share this sitting room so as to form our, er, bond." Miss Lancaster shifted her weight, and Fiona saw the crack in the woman's façade. She was nervous.

Fiona relaxed, for she was nervous too, and it helped to know she wasn't alone. It also helped that her new companion appeared to be just a few years older than her instead of someone with several additional decades. Fiona loved Mrs. Tucket, but it would be nice to have someone young to talk to. "How old are you, Miss Lancaster?"

"Twenty-five."

"Is that the age of most companions in London?"

"Er, yes?" Miss Lancaster sounded uncertain.

"You don't know? I thought Lord Overton said you were an experienced chaperone."

"Oh, of course. Just not here in London." Miss Lancaster abruptly turned. "Come, I'll show you your room. I'm sure your anxious to see it."

"Thank you, I should like that very much, Miss Lancaster."

The taller woman looked back over her shoulder. "Please call me Prudence."

"All right, but you must call me Fiona then. Especially if we're to be friends." How she hoped they would be friends. Fiona hadn't had one in a very long time. Not since Abigail Harding had moved to Ludlow after getting married four years ago.

Prudence's gaze softened and some of the tension seemed to leave her frame. "I would like that."

"Wonderful." Fiona grinned and then gasped as she stepped into her bedchamber. It was more than twice as large as the one in their cottage in Bitterley on her cousin's estate, perhaps three times actually, and decorated in beautiful rose and gold. There was a large bed, a writing desk, a dressing table, and a grand armoire along with smaller dressers for her things. What she owned wouldn't fill even a quarter of everything, but then she supposed her new wardrobe would.

Turning to face Prudence, she clasped her hands together. "I have so many questions, but let me start by asking, when can we go to Bond Street?" There were so many things Fiona was eager to do and experience. Why not start with something close?

"I'm not sure, but soon. His lordship said you would require a wardrobe for the Marriage Mart."

Halfway to the dressing table, Fiona stopped. If the earl thought she was a biddable young lady eager for the marital yoke, he was going to be quite shocked.

Fiona would try not to be amused.

# ALSO BY DARCY BURKE

The Duke of Seduction

The Duke of Kisses

The Duke of Distraction

*The Untouchables: The Spitfire Society*

Never Have I Ever with a Duke

A Duke is Never Enough

A Duke Will Never Do

*Love is All Around*

*(A Regency Holiday Trilogy)*

The Red Hot Earl

The Gift of the Marquess

Joy to the Duke

*Wicked Dukes Club*

One Night for Seduction by Erica Ridley

One Night of Surrender by Darcy Burke

One Night of Passion by Erica Ridley

One Night of Scandal by Darcy Burke

One Night to Remember by Erica Ridley

One Night of Temptation by Darcy Burke

*Secrets and Scandals*

Her Wicked Ways

His Wicked Heart

To Seduce a Scoundrel

To Love a Thief (a novella)

Never Love a Scoundrel

Scoundrel Ever After

*Legendary Rogues*

The Legend of a Rogue

Lady of Desire

Romancing the Earl

Lord of Fortune

Captivating the Scoundrel

**Contemporary Romance**

*Ribbon Ridge*

Where the Heart Is (a prequel novella)

Only in My Dreams

Yours to Hold

When Love Happens

The Idea of You

When We Kiss

You're Still the One

*Ribbon Ridge: So Hot*

So Good

So Right

So Wrong

# ABOUT THE AUTHOR

Darcy Burke is the USA Today Bestselling Author of sexy, emotional historical and contemporary romance. Darcy wrote her first book at age 11, a happily ever after about a swan addicted to magic and the female swan who loved him, with exceedingly poor illustrations. Join her Reader Club newsletter for the latest updates from Darcy.

A native Oregonian, Darcy lives on the edge of wine country with her guitar-strumming husband, incredibly talented artist daughter, and imaginative son who will almost certainly out-write her one day (that may be tomorrow). They're a crazy cat family with two Bengal cats, a small, fame-seeking cat named after a fruit, an older rescue Maine Coon with attitude to spare, and a collection of neighbor cats who hang out on the deck and occasionally venture inside. You can find Darcy at a winery, in her comfy writing chair balancing her laptop and a cat or three, folding laundry (which she loves), or binge-watching TV with the family. Her happy places are Disneyland, Labor Day weekend at the Gorge, Denmark, and anywhere in the UK—so long as her family is there too. Visit Darcy online at www.darcyburke.com and follow her on social media.

facebook.com/DarcyBurkeFans
twitter.com/darcyburke
instagram.com/darcyburkeauthor
pinterest.com/darcyburkewrites
goodreads.com/darcyburke
bookbub.com/authors/darcy-burke
amazon.com/author/darcyburke

## THE UNTOUCHABLES: THE SPITFIRE SOCIETY SERIES
### NEVER HAVE I EVER WITH A DUKE

"Never have I ever given my heart so fast . . . an enticing addiction that stays on your mind and in your heart long after the story is through."

*– Hopeless Romantic*

'There was such a fabulous build-up to Arabella and Graham's first kiss that when they finally give in to it I wanted to high five somebody.'

*– DragonRose Books Galore Reviews*

### A DUKE IS NEVER ENOUGH

"I loved Phoebe and Marcus! Whether as individuals or together, they are just wonderful on the page. Their banter was delightful, and watching two people who are determined not to start a relationship do exactly that was a whole lot of fun."

*– Becky on Books....and Quilts*

"I love the passion between Marcus and Phoebe and not just the steamy bedroom scenes they had, but the passionate nature of their relationship. Their feelings for each other went far past that of just the physical even if they didn't realize it."

*– DragonRose Books Galore Reviews*

## A DUKE WILL NEVER DO

"I have wanted to see Anthony's story since we first met him in The Duke of Distraction from the Untouchables series. He just begged to have a warm, loving, and very caring lady to heal his heart and soul, and he certainly found her in Jane."

*– Flippin' Pages Book Reviews*

"How they care for each other, how they heal each other and hurt each other simultaneously is the very heart and soul of this intriguing story."

*– The Reading Café*

## THE UNTOUCHABLES SERIES

## THE FORBIDDEN DUKE

"I LOVED this story!!" 5 Stars

*-Historical Romance Lover*

"This is a wonderful read and I can't wait to see what comes next in this amazing series..." 5 Stars

*-Teatime and Books*

## THE DUKE of DARING

"You will not be able to put it down once you start. Such a good read."

*-Books Need TLC*

"An unconventional beauty set on life as a spinster meets the one man who might change her mind, only to find his painful past makes it impossible to love. A wonderfully emotional journey from attraction, to friendship, to a love that conquers all."

-Bronwen Evans, *USA Today* Bestselling Author

## THE DUKE of DECEPTION

"...an enjoyable, well-paced story ... Ned and Aquilla are an engaging, well-matched couple – strong, caring and compassionate; and ...it's easy to believe that they will continue to be happy together long after the book is ended."

*-All About Romance*

"This is my favorite so far in the series! They had chemistry from the moment they met...their passion leaps off the pages."

*-Sassy Book Lover*

## THE DUKE of DESIRE

"Masterfully written with great characterization...with a

flourish toward characters, secrets, and romance... Must read addition to "The Untouchables" series!"

*-My Book Addiction and More*

"If you are looking for a truly endearing story about two people who take the path least travelled to find the other, with a side of 'YAH THAT'S HOT!' then this book is absolutely for you!"

*-The Reading Café*

## THE DUKE of DEFIANCE

"This story was so beautifully written, and it hooked me from page one. I couldn't put the book down and just had to read it in one sitting even though it meant reading into the wee hours of the morning."

*-Buried Under Romance*

"I loved the Duke of Defiance! This is the kind of book you hate when it is over and I had to make myself stop reading just so I wouldn't have to leave the fun of Knighton's (aka Bran) and Joanna's story!"

*-Behind Closed Doors Book Review*

## THE DUKE of DANGER

"The sparks fly between them right from the start... the HEA is certainly very hard-won, and well-deserved."

*-All About Romance*

"Another book hangover by Darcy! Every time I pick a favorite in this series, she tops it. The ending was perfect and made me want more."

*-Sassy Book Lover*

## THE DUKE of ICE

"Each book gets better and better, and this novel was no exception. I think this one may be my fave yet! 5 out 5 for this reader!"

*-Front Porch Romance*

"An incredibly emotional story...I dare anyone to stop reading once the second half gets under way because this is intense!"

*-Buried Under Romance*

## THE DUKE of RUIN

"This is a fast paced novel that held me until the last page."

*-Guilty Pleasures Book Reviews*

" ...everything I could ask for in a historical romance... impossible to stop reading."

*-The Bookish Sisters*

## THE DUKE of LIES

"THE DUKE OF LIES is a work of genius! The characters

are wonderfully complex, engaging; there is much mystery, and so many, many lies from so many people; I couldn't wait to see it all uncovered."

*-Buried Under Romance*

"..the epitome of romantic [with]...a bit of danger/action. The main characters are mature, fierce, passionate, and full of surprises. If you are a hopeless romantic and you love reading stories that'll leave you feeling like you're walking on clouds then you need to read this book or maybe even this entire series."

*-The Bookish Sisters*

## THE DUKE of SEDUCTION

"There were tears in my eyes for much of the last 10% of this book. So good!"

*-Becky on Books...and Quilts*

"An absolute joy to read... I always recommend Darcy!"

-Brittany and Elizabeth's Book Boutique

## THE DUKE of KISSES

"Don't miss this magnificent read. It has some comedic fun, heartfelt relationships, heartbreaking moments, and horrifying danger."

*-The Reading Café*

"...my favorite story in the series. Fans of Regency romances will definitely enjoy this book."

## THE DUKE of DISTRACTION

"Count on Burke to break a heart as only she can. This couple will get under the skin before they steal your heart."

"Darcy Burke never disappoints. Her storytelling is just so magical and filled with passion. You will fall in love with the characters and the world she creates!"

## LOVE IS ALL AROUND SERIES

## THE RED HOT EARL

"Ash and Bianca were such absolutely loveable characters who were perfect for one another and so deserving of love... an un-put-downable, sensitive, and beautiful romance with the perfect combination of heart and heat."

"Everyone loves a good underdog story and . . . Burke sets out to inspire the soul with a powerful tale of heartwarming proportions. Words fail me but emotions drown me in the most delightful way."

**THE GIFT OF THE MARQUESS**

"This is a truly heartwarming and emotional story from beginning to end!"

"You could see how much they loved each other and watching them realizing their dreams was joyful to watch!!"

## JOY TO THE DUKE

"...I had to wonder how this author could possibly redeem and reform Calder. Never fear – his story was wonderfully written and his redemption was heart-warming."

"I think this may be my favorite in this series! We finally find out what turned Calder so cold and the extent of that will surprise you."

## WICKED DUKES CLUB Series

## ONE NIGHT OF SURRENDER

"Together, Burke and Ridley have crafted a delightful

"world" with swoon-worthy men, whip-smart ladies, and the perfect amount of steam for this romance reader."

*–Dream Come Review*

"…Burke makes this wonderfully entertaining tale of fated lovers a great and rocky ride."

*–The Reading Café*

## ONE NIGHT OF SCANDAL

"… a well-written, engaging romance that kept me on my toes from beginning to end."

*–Keeper Bookshelf*

"Oh lord I read this book in one sitting because I was too invested."

*–Beneath the Covers Blog*

## ONE NIGHT OF TEMPTATION

"One Night of Temptation is a reminder of why I continue to be a Darcy Burke fan. Burke doesn't write damsels in distress."

*– Hopeless Romantic*

"Darcy has done something I've not seen before and made the hero a rector and she now has me wanting more! Hugh is nothing like you expect him to be and you will love him the minute he winks."

## Secrets & Scandals Series

### HER WICKED WAYS

"A bad girl heroine steals both the show and a highway-man's heart in Darcy Burke's deliciously wicked debut."

–Courtney Milan, *NYT* Bestselling Author

"…fast paced, very sexy, with engaging characters."

–*Smexybooks*

### HIS WICKED HEART

"Intense and intriguing. Cinderella meets *Fight Club* in a historical romance packed with passion, action and secrets."

–Anna Campbell, *Seven Nights in a Rogue's Bed*

"A romance…to make you smile and sigh…a wonderful read!"

–*Rogues Under the Covers*

### TO SEDUCE a SCOUNDREL

"Darcy Burke pulls no punches with this sexy, romantic page-turner. Sevrin and Philippa's story grabs you from the first scene and doesn't let go. *To Seduce a Scoundrel* is simply delicious!"

–Tessa Dare, *NYT* Bestselling Author

"I was captivated on the first page and didn't let go until this glorious book was finished!"

*–Romancing the Book*

## TO LOVE a THIEF

"With refreshing circumstances surrounding both the hero and the heroine, a nice little mystery, and a touch of heat, this novella was a perfect way to pass the day."

*–The Romanceaholic*

"A refreshing read with a dash of danger and a little heat. For fans of honorable heroes and fun heroines who know what they want and take it."

*-The Luv NV*

## NEVER LOVE a SCOUNDREL

"I loved the story of these two misfits thumbing their noses at society and finding love." Five stars.

*–A Lust for Reading*

"A nice mix of intrigue and passion...wonderfully complex characters, with flaws and quirks that will draw you in and steal your heart."

*–BookTrib*

## SCOUNDREL EVER AFTER

"There is something so delicious about a bad boy, no matter what era he is from, and Ethan was definitely delicious."

*-A Lust for Reading*

"I loved the chemistry between the two main characters...Jagger/Ethan is not what he seems at all and neither is sweet society Miss Audrey. They are believably compatible."

-Confessions of a College Angel

### LEGENDARY ROGUES SERIES

## LADY of DESIRE

"A fast-paced mixture of adventure and romance, very much in the mould of *Romancing the Stone* or *Indiana Jones*."

*-All About Romance*

"...gave me such a book hangover! ...addictive...one of the most entertaining stories I've read this year!"

*-Adria's Romance Reviews*

## ROMANCING the EARL

"Once again Darcy Burke takes an interesting story and...turns it into magic. An exceptionally well-written book."

"...A fast paced story that was exciting and interesting. This is a definite must add to your book lists!"

## LORD of FORTUNE

"I don't think I know enough superlatives to describe this book! It is wonderfully, magically delicious. It sucked me in from the very first sentence and didn't turn me loose— not even at the end ..."

"If you love a deep, passionate romance with a bit of mystery, then this is the book for you!"
    -Teatime and Books

## CAPTIVATING the SCOUNDREL

"I am in absolute awe of this story. Gideon and Daphne stole all of my heart and then some. This book was such a delight to read."

"Darcy knows how to end a series with a bang! Daphne and Gideon are a mix of enemies and allies turned lovers that will have you on the edge of your seat at every turn."

**Contemporary Romance**

A contemporary family saga featuring the Archer family of sextuplets who return to their small Oregon wine country town to confront tragedy and find love...

The "multilayered plot keeps readers invested in the story line, and the explicit sensuality adds to the excitement that will have readers craving the next Ribbon Ridge offering."

*-Library Journal* Starred Review on YOURS TO HOLD

"Darcy Burke writes a uniquely touching and heart-warming series about the love, pain, and joys of family as well as the love that feeds your soul when you meet "the one.""

*-The Many Faces of Romance*

I can't tell you how much I love this series. Each book gets better and better.

*-Romancing the Readers*

"Darcy Burke's Ribbon Ridge series is one of my all-time favorites. Fall in love with the Archer family, I know I did."

*-Forever Book Lover*

**RIBBON RIDGE: SO HOT**

**SO GOOD**

" ...worth the read with its well-written words, beautiful descriptions, and likeable characters...they are flirty, sexy and a match made in wine heaven."

-*Harlequin Junkie* Top Pick

"I absolutely love the characters in this book and the families. I honestly could not put it down and finished it in a day."

-*Chin Up Mom*

## SO RIGHT

"This is another great story by Darcy Burke. Painting pictures with her words that make you want to sit and stare at them for hours. I love the banter between the characters and the general sense of fun and friendliness."

-*The Ardent Reader*

" ...the romance is emotional; the characters are spirited and passionate... "

-*The Reading Café*

## SO WRONG

"As usual, Ms. Burke brings you fun characters and witty banter in this sweet hometown series. I loved the dance between Crystal and Jamie as they fought their attraction."

-*The Many Faces of Romance*

"I really love both this series and the Ribbon Ridge series from Darcy Burke. She has this way of taking your heart and ripping it right out of your chest one second and then the next you are laughing at something the characters are doing."

-*Romancing the Readers*

CPSIA information can be obtained
at www.ICGtesting.com
Printed in the USA
BVHW090805041022
648621BV00010B/997